# JOHN PENNEY

Copyright © 2023 John Penney.
All Rights Reserved

Cover Art by Teguh Suwanda
Edited by Tod Clark
Interior Formatting & Design by Sean Duregger

The characters and events in this book are fictitious. Any similarity to real persons, living, dead or undead is coincidental and not intended by the author.

No part of this book may be reproduced in any form or by any electronic or mechanical means, including information storage and retrieval systems, without permission in writing from the publisher, except by a reviewer who may quote brief passages in a review.

Encyclopocalypse Publications
www.encyclopocalypse.com

# CHAPTER ONE

Alison Cutter's eyes snapped open. She looked over at the glowing red clock on her nightstand. It was 3:30. She lay for a moment on her side, giving her groggy mind a chance to focus. Why was she awake in the middle of the night?

The dark room was still. Deathly quiet. Alison rolled over the other way, stretching her arm out for her husband.

"Ray?"

The bed on the other side was empty. Nothing but rumpled covers. Alison took another moment to focus, then slowly sat up. She swept her dark hair from her eyes.

"Ray?... Baby?" There was no answer. Alison's expression darkened. Where did he go? She slowly untangled her long, slender legs from the sheets and dropped her feet to the berber carpet. She sat for a moment on the edge of the bed, scanning her shadowy, contemporary California bedroom. Everything was in place.

Alison coughed to shake off a dry tickle in her throat, and looked across the dark room at her reflection in the dresser mirror. Effortlessly beautiful with a narrow nose and gracefully long chin, her face held perfectly balanced dark eyebrows that framed her deep green eyes. But there was also a sadness that seemed to permanently linger on her thirty-four year old face. It was sadness that had settled deep within her seven years ago and had never left.

*Why am I awake?*

Alison slowly rose , tugged on her over-sized t-shirt and padded slowly to the bedroom door. She paused again, taking in the moment. Something wasn't right. She reached out and pushed open the bedroom door.

The hallway was dark. Empty. Pale light streamed in from the far end near the kitchen. Alison took a silent step out the door, and then she heard voices.

Or something that sounded like voices. They were hushed, low, and murmured. One purred deeply like a grown man, but the other was higher, soft and shallow. First there was one, then the other. A conversation of some kind... But how could that be? It didn't make any sense.

Alison stepped slowly down the dark hall. The family pictures that lined the walls emerged from the dark shadows as she passed them. They were pictures of her life in happier times. Her husband... Their son... Sunny backyard pictures. Stiff, buttoned down professional portraits. Wedding pictures. They lingered now as taunting, cruel reminders of the life that had vanished seven years ago. But they remained defiantly. To take them down would admit the ultimate defeat.

Alison wasn't looking at them this time as she passed. She was looking straight at the faded blue bedroom door halfway down the hall. The door with a faded collage of stickers. Star Wars stickers. Harry Potter stickers. The door to a child's bedroom.

Danny's room.

The muffled, murmured voices swelled slightly louder as she grew closer to the door. Alison finally paused just outside. Her breath involuntarily halted so that she could listen intently... Yes. There. The voices again. They were definitely coming from inside. She leaned forward, straining to hear. The low murmured voice hummed once again. It sounded like Ray. Alison waited for the higher voice to respond again. A few seconds passed.... Then a few more. There was no high voice. Alison slowly exhaled.

She stared for a moment at Danny's door. In the weeks and months after it had happened, she had gone into that room and cried herself to sleep on the narrow little bed. When she woke up again, she cried all over until she fell asleep. The pattern repeated itself throughout those first long and agonizing nights. Ray had always been the strong one. She called it strong but really he was just as shell-shocked as she was. He had just managed to wall himself off from it all. Wall himself off from her. Alison thought that the bottom of the pit was when they lost Danny... But it wasn't. The real bottom came when Ray moved out and they separated for those six months.

The low murmured voice rose again from inside the room. It was definitely Ray. Was he inside mourning the way she had done?... Alison suddenly felt for him. She leaned up close to the door and raised her voice, "Ray?"

The murmured voice instantly stopped.

And then there was silence again. The same deathly stillness that she had felt when she had awoken. A chill tremored through Alison. Surly he just heard her. Why wasn't he answering? She forced her hand to rise from her side and slowly reach for the doorknob. Her fingers stretched out toward the glossy brass orb. She felt the cool metal on her fingertips as she touched it. She hesitated again. Waited. Still nothing. Just silence. Her fingers slowly tightened on the knob, pressing into the slippery cold metal. She gave a twist.

*Click.* The knob hit the mechanism inside. She slowly twisted it the other direction. *Click.* Same thing. The door was locked. Alison stared at the door not sure what to do. The moment stretched in time. And still there was nothing. Just the deathly stillness and the silence. Alison slowly withdrew her hand.

And that's when there was something else.

The sound of buzzing flies. It was a discord that didn't make any sense.

*Flies? Why would there be?...*

An intense rotting odor singed her nostrils. It was vile and deathly. Alison involuntarily choked and covered her nose and mouth. She jerked back from the door and her bare foot splashed into something beneath her. She looked down. In the dim, pale light that streamed from the kitchen down the hall, she saw the rotting, lumpy blood that puddled out from under the crack in the closed door.

Alison's racing mind tried to make sense of jarring sensory overload. What was all this? The odor burned down her throat and her eyes watered. She staggered back from the door as she felt a wave of nausea rise up from an involuntary spasm in her stomach. She gagged and stumbled further back, her bare feet slipping on the rotting slime. She slammed hard against the far wall, then twisted and pushed herself away. The rising bile from her stomach caught in her throat and she choked it back, gasping in more of the repulsive air. This time she couldn't stop it. She vomited. The bitter liquid splashed on the floor, just missing her bare feet. She forced herself further down the hallway, desperately trying to find clean air.

She reached the edge of the kitchen and inhaled again. This time it was better. She staggered to the island in the middle of the shadowy room and wiped the tears from her eyes. She spotted her cell phone next to the tea kettle and reached for it. As she was lifting it to her face, she saw an impossible sight.

A mid-thirties nude man stood in the open refrigerator door, drinking from a carton of milk. His skin was pale and drawn tight against his sinewy frame.

*Tom.*

Alison froze. Her mind scrambled desperately to process the strange sight. Part of what she was seeing made sense; she had seen Tom standing like this before in their kitchen, but the fact he was standing there tonight made no sense at all. He had been out of her life for over a year. It had been a desperate but ultimately doomed relationship she had thrown herself into when she and Ray had been separated for those six long months. Tom was a strikingly handsome but deeply troubled man who had captured her attention and triggered an intense physical affair that had started as abruptly as it had ended.

The overwhelming guilt she felt over the affair and what he had done to himself when she ended it overpowered any remote sense of nostalgia. She had pushed Tom far out of her mind. So why was she dreaming all this?

"Shhh... don't wanna wake your husband," Tom said as he smiled at her in the pale light from the open refrigerator. "Ready for another round?" His voice was warm and intimate. This wasn't a dream. It was real. Tom was standing right in front of her.

"How did... What are you doing here?" Alison could hear the words coming out of her mouth even though the question seemed so impossible.

"Don't fight this, Alison. We both know what you really want."

Alison slowly shook her head, the guilt swallowing her alive "No... no, I—"

*CRACK!*

A wet percussive sound suddenly came from Alison's chest. She looked down, puzzled.

A steel blade from a kitchen knife protruded through her from behind. Blood dripped off the glossy tip. Alison stared as if she was looking at this from somewhere far away. And then—

*Crack! Crack! Crack!* Three more blades shot through her torso from behind. A surge of blood pushed out from the wounds and spread across her t-shirt. An intense burning feeling shot through her body like electricity.

And then she collapsed to the floor.

# CHAPTER TWO

The moon-less night sky over Joshua Tree National Park had a shimmering energy all its own. The strange and twisted silhouettes of the spongy Joshua trees below distorted by the parasitic beetles that thrive within them and the outcroppings of shadowy, wind-worn monzonite rock formations gave the landscape an otherworldly feel. The near-silence was occasionally punctuated by the tortured howls of coyotes giving testament to the difficulty of survival in this hostile world.

And then there was the sound of a car engine.

It was revved high and straining in the thin, dry air. Headlights stabbed over the horizon. The twin lights from the old Dodge bobbed and swung wildly with each depression and curve in the rutted dirt road that they gradually revealed in the inky terrain. Seconds later, the oscillating sounds of a siren joined in, followed by the appearance of flickering blue and red lights through the cloud of dust in the Dodge's wake.

It was a desperate high-speed pursuit that seemed to have taken an unlikely turn into this desolate landscape.

Inside the Yucca Valley police squad car, Officer Arnie Bright squinted through the dust and wrestled with the steering wheel that shimmied and jerked in his grip. Arnie was late forties, stocky with white hair, who spoke with a faded Boston accent; the picture perfect favorite uncle type. Next to him was Jim Briggs, an early thirties ruggedly handsome officer who gripped the radio mic with white knuckles as he spoke. "That's affirmative. Off road in Joshua Tree. Just inside the West entrance off Yucca Mesa Drive."

"Ten four. Proceed with extreme caution. Suspect is armed and dangerous. Repeat – Armed and dangerous," the voice on the radio crackled back.

Jim and Arnie had gotten the APB call about twenty minutes ago on their way back from the BBQ place on 29. Normally Yucca Valley's finest patrol by themselves but, Jim and Arnie just happened to be together because they were on dinner break. As recently as a few years ago, they tried to increase the budget to allow two patrolmen in a car all the time, but the city council shot it down. The crime levels didn't warrant it, they had decided. They were just a small town west of Twenty Nine Palms. A wide spot on the highway filled with big box stores like Best Buy, Target and countless fast food places and gas stations mainly serving the tourists that came their way for the park. They weren't like Twenty Nine Palms that was further east with the military base. Twenty Nine Palms had a slightly bigger force to deal with the jar heads that would go out on benders on the weekend, especially during the wars when their ranks had swollen.

So the APB call had seemed out of place for Yucca Valley. Jim and Arnie had even made Charlotte repeat herself and then asked for details. She told them it had come in from "down below." Usually, there's very little connection between the high desert towns and the rest of the world "down below" but when Charlotte told them that the suspect had been last spotted down in Desert Hot Springs, they were put on alert.

Sure enough, ten minutes later when they had stopped on their way back to the station for some coffee at AM-PM, Jim spotted the suspect's car speed past on the highway. Arnie was on his way back with his coffee when Jim waved him over. Jim hadn't seen Arnie move so fast since he was stealing second base in the Policemen's League game last May down in Palm Springs. He even tossed his precious coffee as he jumped behind the wheel. At first they raced down 29 on a code four - no lights - just so they could gain some ground on him. When they finally reached Yucca Mesa road they were close enough to make the plates and that's when they lit up the Christmas lights and the wild ride began. The perp floored it, skidded off the highway and went up toward the west park entrance. Jim got off on the surge of adrenaline as the high-speed pursuit began. Arnie was just glad he wasn't alone to have to deal with this headache.

And now the two of them were careening down this godforsaken dirt road, trying to catch a suspect that was "armed and dangerous." So much for the low crime rates in Yucca Valley not warranting two officers per car. Jim suddenly stabbed his finger at the road ahead when he saw a large boulder zooming up at them in the dusty light on the right side of the— "Left... Left! *LEFT!*"

Arnie cut the wheel hard to the left, narrowly avoiding the boulder. They swerved into the soft sand on the shoulder. Arnie kept a steady pressure on the accelerator. He knew better than to let up; they needed the momentum or they'd get stuck. Sure enough, he made it back onto the hardpacked dirt road and he exhaled, relieved. But Jim wasn't considering the little victory at all. The Dodge had momentarily dipped below the horizon and was out of sight. "Shit! Go! Go! Go!"

———

Alison's husband Ray Cutter squinted through the dusty windshield of his old Dodge as it careened down through the desert landscape. He was a mid-forties man with salt and pepper hair and premature wrinkles on his weathered face.

*Focus. Focus. Focus.*

Focus on the road. Focus on where he was going. Focus on what he had to do. But as hard as he tried, it was nearly impossible to stop his racing mind as fragments of chaos flew at him from so many different directions. It had all spiraled out of control so fast. It wasn't supposed to go like this. He had come this way for a reason and now he just needed to get where he was going. At first he had tried to find out which police department the car that was following him was from, but he couldn't make it out. That's when he panicked. The wrong police force and it was all over. Now it was too late. He felt like he was swept up in white water rapids, barely keeping his head above water and fighting to avoid wrecking on the rocks. Like everything else that had happened that night.

*Alison. Dear God, Alison... Why? What have I done?*

KABANG!

The car shuddered violently underneath Ray as it bottomed out on something in the deeply rutted road. He fought the wheel as it whipped violently back and forth, but it was no use. The Dodge careened wildly off the dirt road, smashing over rocks and brush and finally crashed to a stop against a Joshua tree in a billow of dust. Ray slapped his head hard against the air bag that came shooting up at him. The engine chugged and went dead. Ray winced in pain and opened his eyes, disoriented. The approaching siren snapped him back to the matter at hand.

The backpack. He couldn't leave the backpack.

He shoved the airbag away, reached over and grabbed the backpack that had been propelled off the front seat and now lay on the floor next to him. His fingers fumbled for the door latch. It was jammed. The sirens grew closer. He looked out the back window and saw the flickering lights glowing through the lingering dust cloud. Ray slid across the front seat to the passenger door and gave a shove. This one opened.

Ray stumbled out of the dead Dodge and slung the backpack over his shoulder. He felt the dull surge of pain in his back from some damage he had done to himself, but he had to push past it. He took off, clambering through the shadowy Joshua trees. His leg snagged on a Cholla and he felt the fiery burn of the fine nettles as they stung his flesh. His leg collapsed beneath him. He stumbled, looked around desperately. He spotted a crevice leading deep between two massive monzonite boulders and hobbled toward it.

The dry night desert air felt like a tendril of cold cotton had been pulled up into Ray's sinuses as he heaved in and out. He reached the entrance to the pitch black crevice between the boulders and hesitated. He looked back and saw the police car skid to a stop by the Dodge. No choice. He pushed himself into the blackness.

The rough monzonite scrapped loudly against the backpack as he moved into the crevice. He adjusted his course, putting his hands out in front of him, feeling for any obstruction that might present itself in front of him. An oppressive stillness settled in the air the deeper he went into the crevice. He could hear his own labored breathing now as it bounced back at him off the rock walls. It was getting narrower. The backpack started scraping against the rough monzonite again but this time he couldn't adjust his trajectory away from it.

Shit. The narrow passage ended abruptly.

Ray grimaced, turned himself around in the tight space and looked back out the entrance. He could see the flickering red and blue lights glowing faintly off the bizarre landscape beyond. The cops were still out there. He couldn't go out. Ray tried to steady his breathing as he pressed back into the darkness. The crackle and squelch of the police radios drifted to him.

He inhaled deeply and closed his eyes. Maybe he'd get lucky. Maybe they'd keep going or look another direction long enough for him to get out of here. He remained silent, listening closely as he slowly exhaled. A moment passed... Then another...

A gentle breeze came swirling down the crevice, it rippled up his arms and across his face. It was cold. Much colder than the desert air and it carried a putrid, rotten odor.

And then he heard it.

A brittle low grinding sound deep from within the rocks.

Ray's eyes snapped open and he looked up. An unnatural deep fissure splintered its way down through the solid monzonite toward him... The rotten black blood oozed out from within.

It had followed him.

It was here.

---

Jim and Arnie swept their flashlights through the twisted forest of Joshua trees as they crept across the uneven terrain. Their guns were drawn. They were ready for anything.

"If this motherfucker's as dangerous as they're saying, we should just seal off this whole goddamn area and get some air support in here from the base," Jim whispered.

"Yeah, probably right. Let's get back to the car and—"

"Don't shoot! Please... I'm here... I'm here... Don't shoot!"

Arnie and Jim spun around, leveling their guns at the panicked man with the wild look in his eyes clutching the backpack.

"Hands in the air!" Jim shouted.

"Drop the backpack," Arnie joined in.

Ray immediately dropped the backpack and cowered to his knees, terrified. "Are you Yucca Valley police?"

"On your stomach!" Jim commanded.

"Please, I'm looking for—" Ray tried again.

"I said on your stomach!" Jim shoved Ray hard. He went down face first into the dust. Arnie kicked the backpack away and trained his pistol on Ray's head as Jim swept Ray's hands behind his back. Ray choked and coughed on the powdery dust, but he didn't give up. He had to tell them. It was his only chance.

"Officer Vale... I'm looking for Officer Vale with the Yucca Valley Police."

# CHAPTER THREE

Officer Bianca Vale pulled her squad car up outside the parking lot security gate at the Yucca Valley police station. It was a two-story cinder block compound on Black Creek Highway at the edge of the town. Aging and ugly, but functional. The high security fence around the back that enclosed the patrol car parking lot made it look almost like a prison. Most people passing out of town wouldn't give it a second look. If it weren't for the plain fluorescent lit sign just off the road that designated it a police station, you'd probably think it was some kind of warehouse.

Bianca pressed the window down and waved her card key at the pad. The gate rumbled open and she pulled inside. She was running a good twenty minutes late for her ten o'clock shift, but she still needed a few more minutes to change out of her date-night dress. At least she had gotten out of her high heels and into her Uggs. She had hoped to get home, but the date had gone long and the guy's house was up on the Mesa. It would have added at least another forty-five minutes to go all the way home and back.

Bianca pulled into an empty space and shut the squad car down. She rattled through her purse, pulled out some Visine and dropped her head back. She squirted a couple drops in each of her large brown eyes, then sat for a moment, blinking back the cool liquid and sighed. Twelve hours. She just had to get through her twelve hour shift and she could crash. She finally pulled her head up, swept her thick tousled chestnut hair up into a ponytail and secured it with a band. She twisted around to grab her uniform pants off the seat, raising her lean legs. She shimmied into the pants, raising her hips with a sudden thrust so she could get them to her waist. She exhaled and collapsed back, still feeling a little dizzy from all the shots of Jack she had earlier that night. She looked out at the dark parking lot to make sure no one was around, then pulled her dress up over her head. The cool air made her bare skin tingle as she quickly grabbed her uniform shirt and pulled it on.

Her cell phone chirped.

Bianca snapped it up from her purse and checked the number. It was her sister. Shit. Bianca deliberated, then decided she could just get it over with a quick, "Hi Sheila."

"I missed you today, Bianca"

"Yeah, you know I'm really sorry. I had to pull a double shift," Bianca said as she buttoned her shirt.

"Oh... Well, my birthday just wasn't the same without you."

Shit. Her birthday. More guilt. Bianca thought fast. "Right. I know. I'm sorry."

"We want you to come see us when you can."

"Yeah, I will. I've got a present for you." Bianca dug into her purse and took out some tissue.

"Well I'm not asking you to come by just to give me a present, silly."

Bianca pulled the visor down and looked into the mirror. God it was cloying when her sister said things like "silly." Cloying and so typical. "No, I know that, Sheila."

"I just want you to come by," Sheila added.

Bianca carefully wiped away her heavy eye-liner. "I will... you know, when I can," Bianca hesitated, studying her reflection. She was pretty by any standard. Large brown eyes, cute upturned nose and a slender jawline. Her olive skin was the perfect shade lighter than her natural chestnut hair color. It was the southern Italian side from her father.

"Mom and Dad were hoping you'd be there. They said you haven't been to see them in a while either."

Of course. There it was. Bianca had to know that was coming. The twinge of guilt flickered in her stomach. The guilt was always brimming just under the surface. The more they tried to pull her back toward them, the worse it became. Bianca snapped the visor back against the roof, annoyed. "I know – I know. Look, I—"

"Are you okay?"

Bianca tossed the tissue away, and made a deliberate attempt to lighten her tone. "Yes. Of course. I'm fine. I'm great."

"I prayed for you today."

Bianca felt the queasy hung-over feeling in her stomach get worse. The edge of the black void was on the horizon again. She wanted to scream at her sister the way she told her that so innocently. How the hell could she not see how brutal she was being? Instead, Bianca took a breath and answered evenly, "Sheila. You don't have to do that, I.."

"I know I don't have to. I want to. The Lord Jesus loves you, Bianca."

Another breath. There was no way out of this. It had to end. "Look, I... I really have to go. Things are getting busy here. Say hi to Mom and Dad for me, okay?"

"I will, of course."

"Good... good thanks," Bianca punched the phone off.

BLEEP! A new text message popped up on her phone. Now what?

Bianca looked down at the glowing words: "Great date. Let's do it again some time. Call me." Bianca stared at the message for a moment. He was a nice enough jar-head from 29 Palms, but all the talk about going to Lake Powell and racing around on his jet skis had gotten old quick. And was it really a date? Maybe, if that's what you call meeting for dinner at Sizzler at five o'clock and then going to his little room on the base afterward. It was exactly what Bianca was looking for, but she never went in thinking it was a real date. It was a hook-up. It was perfect. But that was all.

Bianca finally punched "delete" and pocketed her phone. She grabbed her purse and opened the car door. A light breeze kicked up from out of the dark desert. It felt good, but it also meant it was going to get a lot colder. Bianca reached back into the car, grabbed her holster and her jacket. She slammed the door and started to the back entrance of the station.

Bianca gazed out at the burnt orange lights of Yucca Valley a mile down the highway. They built the station out this far expecting the town to eventually join it. The Great Recession put a stop to that for a few years but now the plan seemed to be working. There were a couple construction sites between the station and town, mostly for storage unit compounds. That seemed to be the business to be in when you're this close to a military base. At the end of the day, it just meant that they didn't get a lot of traffic past the station, especially after night. Most of the people who lived up Black Creek highway were home and asleep by now and if you didn't live up there, there'd be no reason to head that way.

Bianca reached the back door to the station and stopped. She suddenly found herself just standing there without knowing why...

And then it hit her. The cool breeze had suddenly stopped. Not just died down, but stopped dead. Bianca slowly turned, looked past the dumpster by the fence and out at the dark desert opposite the town lights in the distance. It was unusually quiet and still. Quiet enough to hear rhythmic heavy breathing coming out of the darkness beyond the dumpster.

Bianca slowly reached down and rested her hand on her pistol in her holster. She tried to focus in on the exact direction of the eerie sound as she slowly started toward the dumpster. As she grew closer, a breeze began again... Bianca stopped once more. It was all wrong. The breeze was blowing the opposite direction now. Coming from behind the dumpster. Bianca could feel her heart start to race and her hands tingle as she slowly pulled her pistol out of the holster. She forced herself to continue toward the dumpster. As she cleared the edge, a pair of pale yellow eyes gleamed back at her from the shadows.

Bianca recoiled, frantically clawed for her flashlight and snapped it on. It was a coyote staring back at her from the other side of the fence. Bianca took a shallow breath and steadied her nerves. "Get out of there! Go!"

The coyote didn't move. Instead it locked a steady gaze at Bianca and stood its ground. Bianca tried again, this time waving her hands. "Go! Go!"

But the coyote still didn't move. It just kept staring at her. The moment began to stretch in time... An unsettled feeling began to creep over Bianca; a vague anxiety from deep in her stomach. It began like the feeling she got sometimes late at night when she started to sober up and began regretting what had happened the night before. Usually she just rode the anxiety out, knowing that it would all subside when daylight came.

But then it became different. It became a deeper sense of guilt. The deeper feeling she'd been spending the last seven years drowning out. It was back now with a vengeance in the eyes of that coyote.

Bianca suddenly broke the gaze. She turned quickly and hurried to the back door of the station. Her hand trembled as she ran her key card across the pad and the door buzzed open.

# CHAPTER FOUR

The cluttered bullpen station office was humming with activity. That was unusual here, especially at this hour. Jim was at his desk talking on the phone, "...That's correct. Officer Jim Briggs, Yucca Valley Station requesting a 10-16 prisoner pick up..."

Station Sergeant Benjamin Roberts, a paternal, white-haired 64 year old, was at the next desk over. He was busy logging in the contents from Ray's backpack. He pulled out a wallet, a pair of glasses, a Transformer toy... and finally a primitive handmade artifact of some kind. The circular frame was made from old, small black bones wrapped with what looked like human hair. A five sided star made from the same black bones filled the circle.

The back door down the hall buzzed open, and Bianca breezed in. "Somebody been feeding the coyotes again?"

Benjamin looked up from the primitive symbol. "Don't think so."

"Well they're getting territorial. There's a big ass one by the garbage."

Benjamin set the symbol down as Bianca passed by. "Charlotte's got the perp up on her screen. Take a look at him."

"On my way."

She continued past Jim, who was carefully taking notes as he continued on the phone, "...good, yeah no worries. We'll keep him locked down tight here until you can come up in the morning." Jim looked up and quickly tried to make eye contact with Bianca. But she purposefully avoided him and crossed around behind Arnie's desk. Arnie was carefully typing out the arrest report in his usual two-finger way. Bianca dropped her purse and jacket at her desk and looked over at Charlotte Wagner, the station dispatch officer. Charlotte was 23 years old, African American; small but tough and cute as hell. Charlotte was seated at her dispatch bay in front of a bank of computer screens. The security camera feed from the holding cell was up on her main monitor. Ray could be seen rocking back and forth as he sat on the edge of his cot. Another detainee could be seen in the next cell over, passed out cold on his cot.

Bianca stepped up behind Charlotte, and pointed to Ray on the screen. "That the guy?"

"Ummm hmmm. That's him alright"

Bianca leaned in closer and studied the monitor. "You sure he asked for me?"

"That's what Jim said. But who knows? That perp in there is a whole lotta batshit crazy. Sick fucko sunk seven knives through his wife's heart. I'm downloading the crime scene video from San Bernardino now."

Bianca peered for a moment longer at Ray on the monitor, then crossed back over to Benjamin who was logging in Ray's wallet and glasses. "You get a good look at him?"

"Yeah," Bianca answered.

"And?"

"Never seen him before."

"You sure? Not even socially?"

A smile curled the corner of Bianca's lip. "Please. His age? You know I only date the young sociopaths."

Benjamin returned a smile. "Well, cross check his name with

your arrest records. Make sure you didn't pinch him for some traffic violation."

"Yessir."

"Of course there's always a chance he randomly pulled your name off the internet or some crazy thing. Just check it out thoroughly and put a statement into the report."

"You got it," Bianca said as she picked up the crude, primitive symbol. She turned it over in her hands, examining it carefully. "This is some creepy shit. What is it?"

"Not sure. Dreamcatcher maybe?"

"Not like any dreamcatcher I've ever seen." Bianca set the symbol down and picked up the Transformer toy. She smiled nostalgically, clicked it around and expertly re-configured it into a car. She finally set it down. "What's with all the kid's stuff? He was alone, wasn't he? "

"Yeah. Like I said... he's got a lot of oddball stuff," Benjamin finished putting all of Ray's belongings along with the backpack into a clear evidence pouch and sealed it.

Bianca reached out for the pouch. "Want me to take it down?"

"Would you?"

"Of course." She took the pouch from Benjamin, started to turn, then hesitated. "Hey, I... I'm sorry I'm late."

Benjamin looked up at her. It was a look Bianca had seen from him many times. A paternal look of genuine concern. "Right. About that. You okay?

Bianca managed a reassuring smile in return. "I'm fine."

"I put you on Watch Supervisor tonight. You sure you're up for it?"

"Absolutely."

"I'll be at home. Call me if anything comes up."

"Won't have to. Everything will be just fine here."

Benjamin smiled and looked back at his paperwork. "That's what I like to hear."

Bianca picked up the evidence bag and started back across the office as Jim finished up his call with San Bernardino. "Okay then. We'll expect to see you up here at 0-700." He hung up, sprung to his feet and caught up with Bianca as she reached the back hall. He glanced at the busy office, then lowered his voice intimately. "Where were you?"

Bianca continued into the back hall without making eye contact. "Just running a little late." She knew that's not what he meant, but right now her head was still thumping and her mouth felt like cotton. All this would have to wait until the hangover was on the way out.

"No. I'm talking about earlier."

"What do you mean?"

"You know what I mean."

Bianca threw open the door to the stairwell, stepped inside with Jim on her heels.

"Come on, Bianca. What the hell?"

Bianca took a breath, stopped at the top landing and turned back to him. "You searched the perp, didn't you?"

"Of course."

"You got his belt?"

"Yes."

"Shoe laces too?"

"Why're you busting my balls?"

"I'm Watch Commander tonight."

"So?"

"So I don't want that asshole offing himself before San Bernardino comes to pick him up in the morning."

"I know how to do my job, Bianca."

Bianca turned and started down the stairs. Jim, frustrated, called after her, "he asked for you by name when I arrested him."

"Yeah, I've already been through that with Ben," Bianca called back over her shoulder.

"Hey, Bianca. Wait!"

"We need to get someone back out on patrol. Ask Arnie if he'll go when he's finished with that report," she said as she disappeared around the corner of the basement landing.

"Bianca!" Jim stared after her for a moment, then turned and went back into the office, frustrated.

———

Bianca's standard issue black shoes squeaked on the glossy linoleum as she strode down the empty basement hallway, past the entryway to the holding cells and all the way to the end where the hallway made a turn to the right. She went down a couple more steps into a short hall and finally to the entrance of the evidence room. She fished out her keys and unlocked the deadbolt. The metal door creaked as she shoved it open and snapped on the light. The dim overhead fluorescents flickered to life, illuminating the shadowy rows of steel shelves divided into individual mesh-metal cages filled with boxes and pouches of evidence. The door bumped closed behind Bianca as she crossed down one of the rows, pulled out another key and unlocked an empty compartment. She set the pouch with the backpack inside and closed the little door, carefully locking it again. Bianca paused. It was cool and silent in here. The perfect place to just sit for a while and let her hangover subside. She leaned back against the evidence cage behind her, closed her eyes and rubbed her temples. She knew before the shift was over that she'd have to deal with the "Jim problem." He'd made that perfectly clear. Her best plan was to put it off, stick to the work and maybe at least make it to dinner break. Bianca had perfected the art of making problems just go away by avoiding them, but unfortunately this wasn't one of those times. She had fucked this one up somehow—

The faint sound of ragged exhaled breath drifted to her from the stillness.

Bianca's eyes snapped open. She quickly scanned the shadowy maze of cages around her, trying to find the direction it had come from. But there was nothing now. It was silent. She slowly stepped to the edge of the row, paused again and listened. Still nothing. She remembered that the door had closed behind her but maybe she had missed it opening again somehow. It was worth a try.

"Jim?"

No such luck. No easy way to explain what she had heard. Bianca's heart began to race. What the hell was going on? First the coyote and now this. Was this the price of nursing a hangover... or was it something more? The once safe haven to nurse her hangover suddenly seemed very different. The twisting shadows. The cages filled with personal items from so many past crimes. A million places someone could hide. Bianca swallowed dryly. Was this more of her anxiety bullshit? Bianca waited a few moments longer, then quickly backed up the aisle. She looked both ways, then quickly cut over to the door and pulled it open. She snapped off the light, slipped outside and locked the door.

And now the room was dark once more. Just a very faint pale light glowed from around the door as Bianca's footsteps retreated down the hallway.

After a moment, the unearthly rush of air filled the dark room again. And then—

A dark, wet stain began to form on the backpack; the rotten, clotted blood seeped out through the burlap fabric.

The wound was beginning to ooze.

It was probing... Searching... Testing the weakest link... Trying to find a way through once again.

# CHAPTER FIVE

As Bianca walked back up the main basement hallway, her thoughts turned once again to Ray Cutter, the prisoner who had asked for her by name. Nothing about him had seemed familiar on the security screen, but it was always possible she could have missed some detail that might jog her memory. It was definitely worth a look in person.

She stepped through the entryway to the holding area, rounded the half-wall and the row of cells came into view. There were four basic, functional cells with floor to ceiling white enamel painted iron bars. A drunk middle-aged "John Doe" transient was passed out on the cot in the closest cell. They were hoping to get an I.D. on him if he ever sobered up.

Bianca peered past the two empty middle cells to the one on the far end. She could see Ray's shadowy figure rocking back and forth on the edge of his bunk, partially obscured by the latticework of vertical bars. He was whispering something to himself. Bianca stepped a little closer. Bits of the words became clear to her, but they were nonsensical. "Ne... Nanicawai... demazai... nean... Dua..."

Bianca continued closer still, straining to hear. "Nanichawai... demazai... nean... Dua..." Clearly the words were not English. Not

Spanish. They were something else. Latin maybe? She stopped when she could finally get a clear view of the strange man. His head was bowed and his eyes were closed as he rocked back and forth. Bianca looked him over carefully. Nothing about him looked familiar. Bianca had been right the first time; she had never seen him before.

Bianca finally turned to leave and then— Ray stopped rocking. His eyes snapped open. He cocked his head like a bird and stared off into the darkness... "It's coming..." He whispered. Then, as if he could sense she was staring at him, Ray slowly turned his head. His eyes landed on her, drilling strangely straight into her. "It's very close," He whispered again.

They remained looking at each other for a moment, and then Ray's eyes drifted from Bianca's face down to her name tag. His expression instantly changed.

*There she is. Standing right in front of me.*

Ray leaped up and rushed to the bars. "Officer Vale!"

Bianca recoiled and clawed for her pistol, "Back down. Get back on your cot!"

"No, please! Let me explain!" Ray was very lucid now. Lucid but panicked.

The drunk transient in the other cell rolled over and groaned groggily, "Tryin' to sleep here..."

"We don't have much time!" Ray insisted as he clutched the bars with white knuckles.

"You heard me. Back down!" Bianca unsnapped the safety on her holster.

"Dude, come on. Keep that shit down." The transient implored louder.

"Shut the fuck up," Ray snapped back, annoyed.

"Hey! Both of you. Settle down!" Bianca stepped toward the bars, keeping her hand on her pistol for emphasis.

Ray took a cleansing breath. He lowered his voice, still looking at her intently. "Officer Vale, please... I need you to hear me out. This thing... The one who killed my wife... you know who he is..."

Bianca stood her ground. No matter how many times she had dealt with psych patients, they always managed to unnerve her. She never could seem to indulge them or placate them the way she was supposed to. Instead she kept her guard up and came on strong. "Don't test me asshole. You heard what I said."

"But if you just give me a chance to explain, I—"

"Sit down. Now. Shut up," Bianca insisted slowly. There was a moment of silence, then Ray slowly backed away and took a seat back on his cot.

Bianca remained in her ready stance for a bit longer, then finally turned away. She slowly relaxed her grip on her pistol as she walked steadily toward the door. This evening had started off rough and was getting rougher. She just needed a moment to collect herself. Some aspirin and one of those Monster rehydrating energy drinks would be just the thing to set her straight, she decided. Bianca reached the half wall and was almost out the holding cell entryway, when she heard him say it.

"Henrick Whitfield."

The two words came out of Ray calmly, but they were enough to stop Bianca cold in her tracks. A chill shot straight through her. She froze.

Ray looked over at Bianca. *Thank God.* Even with her back to him he could tell he had reached her. Just as he had hoped he would. He slowly sat up higher and raised his voice, "Now please, Officer... come back... just hear me out."

Ray's imploring words hung in the silence for a moment, but then instead of getting Bianca to turn back, she suddenly continued toward the entrance.

*No Wait! What is she doing?*

Ray shot up from his cot once more. "Officer Vale! Please!"

But she just kept going. Ray was desperate. She couldn't slip away like this. It was all too important. This might be his only chance to try to make her understand. He raced once more to the bars and yelled desperately, "It knows what you did... It'll use it against you!"

But Bianca was gone.

Ray trembled, frustrated. The drunk transient chuckled to himself, "Yeah... yeah... I know what you did too, asshole. And I'm going to use it against you if you don't shut up..."

Ray remained at the bars staring after Bianca. After a moment, he slowly turned. A dark, fatalistic smile curled on his lips as he slowly took his seat once more on the cot. "We're already dead... every one of us."

———

Bianca slammed the door to the small upstairs bathroom and locked it. She quickly threw on the faucet. Her hands trembled as she took out a Xanax and popped it dry in her mouth. Aspirin. Energy drinks. Nothing like that was going to help her now. Xanax. That was what she needed. Possibly even two.

*Henrick Whitfield.*

He had said it. The name.

*Please no... Don't let this be happening.*

Bianca cupped the running water in her shaking hand and slurped it up. She closed her eyes and took a deep breath, waiting for the Xanax to take hold. There had to be a way to make sense of this. Something. Anything.

He was crazy. He was fucking with her. That's what it was. He had read about that horrible summer and now he had come here to fuck with her.

The thought began to bring Bianca back to Earth. Of course she was right. She had to be. It was probably only a matter of time before something like this happened. Bianca's involvement was public knowledge. She had been all over the news. There was no reason he couldn't have seen her or read about her and somehow folded it into his mania in some way.

Bianca finally opened her eyes. She stared at her reflection for a long moment. Even with all the rational explanations, it still didn't make the growing unease in the pit of her stomach subside. It had been awhile, but like a sick old friend, the knot in her stomach had returned. Her heart began to pump normally again. She finally took another deep breath and turned from the mirror.

Benjamin had his jacket over his arm and his lunch pail in his hand as he headed toward the back hall. It had been a long shift and he was glad it was finally over. He was almost to the back door when the bathroom suddenly popped open in front him. Benjamin dodged Bianca as she emerged.

"Shit. Sorry," Bianca said as she quickly closed the bathroom door.

Benjamin smiled and stepped around her. Bianca smiled back, but her effort couldn't really hide her flushed expression. Benjamin hesitated, turned back. "You sure you're okay tonight? I can put Jim or Arnie on Supervisor if you want."

Bianca waved him off, pushed her smile harder. "No. I'll be fine. You go on home." She strode off toward the office bullpen. Benjamin gave her a final look, then fished out his keys and stepped up to the back security door.

Jim and Arnie were at the operations desk, looking over Charlotte's shoulder at the crime scene video that had just arrived. It was surprisingly clear even though it was shot with the S.I.D.'s detective's body cam. The image moved up the hallway and the gruesome scene in the kitchen. The walls, cabinets, and counters were sprayed with blood. Ray's wife was crumpled on the floor with the seven knives sunk through her torso. The S.I.D. detective spoke in a monotone as he detailed the scene, "Blood evidence from ten... eight... six meters from the South end of the kitchen." The image shifted around the body on the floor. "Victim's body facing East. Left hand reaching north, holding the telephone."

Jim winced. "Seven knives. That's some serious acupuncture," he said in a lame attempt at humor.

Bianca stepped up behind the group, her eyes locked on the screen as the image moved around the body, scrutinizing every detail. The voice on the video droned on, "Victim's right hand under her right side pelvis. Head turned facing West. Contusions on left side of the face, most likely as a result of a fall to the floor…"

Charlotte eased back on her screen and shook her head. "What do you say we take this fucknut out back and just shoot him now?"

"Count me in," Jim agreed.

Bianca watched a moment longer, then crossed over to her own desk. She took a seat and clicked open Ray's booking file on her computer. She scanned the details, then highlighted Ray's full legal name: Raymond Arthur Cutter. Bianca then clicked over into a nation-wide law enforcement search engine. She entered his name and social security number, clicked in his fingerprints, then sat back with her eyes glued on the screen as the program went to work. This was the only way to be sure Ray's knowledge of Henrick Whitfield was nothing more than the ranting of a mad man.

As Bianca stared into the fluorescent glow of her screen, there was no way for her to know it was already too late. This night. This police station. These very people. It was a confluence. A confluence begun in the past, brought here by a desperate man in the present… and it would change everything about every one of them forever.

———

Benjamin trudged across the dark security parking lot to his squad car. He opened the back door, tossed his jacket and lunch pail in back. He shoved it closed, then opened the driver's door. He was about to climb in when a stale breeze suddenly rose from the dark desert beyond the security fence. Benjamin slowly turned into the breeze and inhaled. It was a pungent, repulsive, rotting decay. Benjamin coughed hard, turned away and covered his mouth. He was about to get into the car when a faint bestial snarling drifted to him on the breeze. Benjamin immediately snapped his attention back to the dark fence. The snarling grew louder.

The coyote. It had to be the coyote that Bianca had complained about. Benjamin threw the car door closed and started out across the dark lot toward the dumpster, pulling his flashlight as he went. The closer he got, the more intense the acrid smell grew. He scanned his flashlight beam across the dented old dumpster. The snarling sounds grew more intense.

Benjamin finally passed around the edge of the dumpster. His flashlight beam landed on the source of the sounds.

He had been wrong.

It wasn't a single coyote. It was an entire pack now; over a dozen coyotes strong. They were feverishly licking and chewing on the cyclone security fence that was dripping with the lumpy, black rotting blood.

A sick feeling welled up in Benjamin as he took in the orgiastic sight. It was more than just the foul odor, it was the disturbing way the coyotes attacked the fence. They were trembling, licking and compulsively biting as if their bodies were out of their control. Benjamin finally kicked the fence. "Yah!"

The rabid beasts ignored him. Benjamin stayed a moment longer, then finally turned away.

Benjamin quickly returned to his squad car, climbed in and slammed the door. He took a deep breath and exhaled, trying to purge the acrid smell from his lungs. Whatever had leaked onto that fence had to be cleaned; once that was gone, the coyote problem would take care of itself, he reasoned. He'd deal with it first thing in the morning. Now it was time to go home. He was tired and it had been a long day.

Benjamin reached around and pulled on his seatbelt. He put the key in the ignition and gave it a turn. The engine chugged a couple of times. His headlights momentarily flickered on.

*It was right there.*

A looming human-like form was standing in front of his car. Blurry and densely black all at the same time.

The headlights blinked off. Then briefly on again.

The figure was gone.

The engine stalled. The headlights died once more. Benjamin's heart thumped up into his throat.

*What the fuck was that?!*

Benjamin frantically grabbed the flashlight from the seat and clicked it on once more. His mouth was dry and his hand was shaking as he slowly panned it around from his side window, across the windshield and out the passenger window.

The parking lot was empty.

Benjamin remained motionless, his mind racing. *Something was just there. Right there in front of the car.*

A moment passed... Then another... Benjamin slowly got his breathing under control.

*Shit.*

He deliberated his next move. He finally decided he would have to go back inside, turn on the security lights, enlist the others and make a complete search of the back parking lot. That made sense. That was the right thing to do. Benjamin reached over to remove the car keys.

"You didn't listen to me, Benny..."

The frail dry voice was right next to him. Benjamin looked over, startled.

But the seat next to him was empty. Benjamin shot a look in the back seat. Empty too.

The world began to spin. He knew that voice. That old, papery cracking voice. What the hell was going on? The coyotes. That thing outside. And now this...

*My dead mother's voice.*

———

How many times had he felt the anguish, the frustration and the guilt that her voice had brought him? Benjamin made a second look all around the empty car.

*Christ... what the hell? Pull yourself together.*

This couldn't be possible. His mother had been dead now for almost seven years. Benjamin took another cleansing breath. He struggled desperately to stay focused in the present moment, but the memories of those suffocating three years suddenly came flooding back to him.

It had all started innocently enough with a phone call from his sister. Susan had always been in charge of dealing with their mother; she had found the Ojai home to begin with and Benjamin had done his part by turning over a large part of his savings to make it all financially possible. Susan had always been more family-oriented and had stayed in touch with their parents much more than Benjamin ever had. Susan was always the cheerful one, bouncing along through life with a glass half full. But not this time. Not this call. Susan's voice was quaking. She broke down as she told Benjamin that her husband had drained the account over gambling debts. The two of them were separated over the whole nasty thing. As Susan broke down, Benjamin's mind reeled, trying to make sense of this awful news and what it meant to him. And then it hit. Susan told him that she had no place for their mother now that her marriage was in such a state. Benjamin needed to take her in. So what could he say? He knew what he wanted to say. He wanted to tell Susan that he was eighteen months away from retiring and had no room in his future for an addled old woman with dementia. But instead, he cursed her husband and threatened a lawsuit. Of course there really couldn't be a lawsuit without affecting his sister, which was quickly made apparent.

So, Benjamin did what he had done most of his life. He went along. The first several weeks she was living with Benjamin and his wife Eileen had been chaotic. Nights waking up to find his mother wandering in the back yard. Finally they got into a routine, but they quickly lost their weekends. Benjamin couldn't retire and still make ends meet. Everything in their lives had changed with that phone call.

And Benjamin's bitterness grew. He stopped talking to Susan altogether and even made excuses not to be home when she came to visit their mother. The treadmill days and nights ground on and on. Eileen and Benjamin fought more and more. Neither one of them saw any light at the end of this grueling tunnel. The old bitch. The stinking, ugly old bitch. God how angry he got when he thought about it all.

And then there was that day. That sunny, innocuous day. That agonizing black day before the unseen dawn.

Eileen had thrown her back out while trying to move his mother's bed so she couldn't drive his mother to her doctor's appointment. Benjamin had to leave work and cut his lunch hour short to take her. When he showed up at home, he had to single-handedly get his mother dressed and ready. He was already running late. He managed to get her into the car and she started rambling about something. *"I can't do it, Benny. Help me. I can't fasten the belt."* As usual, he didn't pay any attention to her. Instead, he sped away toward her doctor's office.

Benjamin was checking a text message from Eileen when the truck ran the light. It plowed into the passenger side, killing his mother instantly. Then came the blackness. And then came the dawn. Benjamin woke up with a shattered shoulder and several broken ribs...

But he was free.

The guilt didn't set in for several months. He hadn't secured her seatbelt and she had been compressed into the windshield. Her back twisted all the way back and her shattered head dented almost all the way through the safety glass.

Benjamin saw it first in his sister's eyes. The blame. And it wasn't long after that Benjamin felt it too. The words his mother said came back clearer with each passing day. *"I can't do it, Benny. I can't fasten the belt. Help me."* He had ignored her. He was in a hurry.

Guilt grows over time. It can be pushed around and manifested in different ways, but it always comes raging back in the end.

Benjamin sat in his car in the dark parking lot, his heart pounding. He finally pulled his mind back to the matter at hand. He had just seen someone... or something... in the security lot. He needed to go back inside. He reached over for the door handle and then he heard the old voice once more. *"I told you... I couldn't do it... I couldn't fasten it..."*

Benjamin spun, startled, and this time he saw it. His mutilated mother was right there in the passenger seat. Half of her skull was collapsed inward; splinters of bone and brain spilled down her old blood-soaked nightgown. Her back was bent in that odd, twisted way it had ended up in the accident with the seatbelt cutting deep across the base of her neck.

*"Benny... Benny, why?"*

Pangs of guilt stabbed deep into his soul. The world collapsed in on itself. Why was this happening? Why was he seeing this? Benjamin closed his eyes tightly. Fighting to make the image go away. He trembled as he reached down to un-click his seatbelt.

But the latch was jammed.

Benjamin began to hyperventilate. He squeezed his eyes closed tighter as his sweaty fingers fumbled with the belt latch. He just needed to get out. Now. If he opened his eyes, he might see her again. He dug his fingers into the edge of the latch and pulled with all his might. Still no luck. The stubborn latch wouldn't open.

*"Goddamnit!"*

And then the seatbelt began to tighten around him.

Benjamin immediately opened his eyes. He looked down at the constricting belt, astonished, as it moved by some unseen force around his torso.

A jolt of adrenaline shot through Benjamin and he started thrashing violently back and forth, thrusting all his weight into the tightening belt. But the belt just kept getting tighter and tighter. The shoulder strap cut deeper and deeper into his neck, just like it had on his mother. He reached up and clawed desperately, trying to pry it away from his throat. But he couldn't do it.

There was a sickening fleshy pop as the belt ripped deep into his carotid artery. Dark crimson blood washed down his chest.

Benjamin twitched spastically...

And then slumped over, dead.

# CHAPTER SIX

**T**he crime scene footage on Charlotte's screen suddenly glitched. "What the fuck is this?" Charlotte reached down, checked the power cord to the monitor. It was secure in the power strip. And then it happened again.

Over at Bianca's desk, the screen glitched too, but she was far too engrossed in what she was reading to pay any attention. The words on the screen seemed unreal. Bianca took a shaky breath and read them again, carefully. Slowly this time. Everything suddenly seemed to stand still. She could feel the spaces between each of her heartbeats. The words on the screen had suddenly changed everything for her.

Jim looked over and saw Bianca at her desk, staring at her monitor with a shell-shocked look on her face. "Bianca?"

Bianca remained frozen. Charlotte and Arnie saw Jim's concerned expression and looked over too. Now they were all puzzled. Jim tried again, louder this time, "Bianca, you okay?"

Bianca suddenly pushed away from her desk and walked away without answering. Charlotte shot a curious look at Jim, "What's with her?" Charlotte's question hung in the air for a moment.

Jim slowly crossed over to Bianca's desk and looked down at her monitor. He perused the summation of Ray Cutter's life, and a detail suddenly jumped off the screen. "No... shit," he muttered.

Charlotte and Arnie exchanged a look and then joined Jim at Bianca's desk. "What the hell is going on?"

Jim slowly looked up at them. "Our prisoner. That guy in there... His son was killed... murdered... by the Bathtub Butcher."

Arnie drew a tight breath. "Oh Jesus... Are you serious?" He quickly started reading the details on Bianca's screen.

Charlotte was clearly out of the loop. "What's a Bathtub Butcher?"

"Henrick Whitfield," Arnie answered.

Charlotte shook her head vaguely. "Yeah?"

Arnie looked up at her once more. "Before your time. About five years ago he terrorized the Inland Empire. Bianca was working the case when she was down in Palm Springs. Anyway, when they finally tracked him down and surrounded his house he killed himself... and when they went in, they found the remains of a dozen... kids."

Across the bullpen in the break room, Bianca carefully poured a cup of coffee with her shaking hands. She looked back out at Jim, Charlotte and Arnie at her desk. She could tell by Charlotte's expression what Jim was telling her. Bianca looked away again, placed the coffee pot back on the burner. She focused in on her coffee cup as she carefully set it on the counter and reached for a sugar pack. Her every move became slow and deliberate. Her fingers slowly tore open the pouch. The white granules slid into the dark steaming liquid. The details suddenly became very important. A comfortable bit of normal; a way she could ground herself as she felt the entire world around her slowly sliding into Hell. The man in the cell had conjured up more than a painful memory. His warning suddenly became extremely threatening. It was clear now. Someway, somehow, it was happening.

*The monster has once again entered my life.*

The thought stabbed loudly into her mind, abruptly ending her attempt to deny it. She closed her eyes and suddenly found herself back there. She felt the sting from the dusty desert breeze as they surrounded the monster's house. She felt the pang of adrenaline when they finally moved in. Everything she had been working so desperately on was about to come to an end. All the months of obsession she had spent on the case trying to find the monster. The sleepless days and nights. Everyone on her team knew it was personal to her and they stood by her, working just as hard. There was nothing Bianca wanted more in the world that day than to enter the monster's place and find her niece alive and well. In the rare quiet moments leading up to that day, she had convinced herself that she was prepared for the worst. After all, her niece had been missing six weeks and Bianca had dealt first hand with the harsh realities of missing persons reports before. But even though she had convinced herself she was being realistic, nothing had prepared her for what she had found inside. Dark, hideous evil exists in the world. But it doesn't appear on a dark, stormy night. It appears on a bright, sunny day in a run-down shack at the end of a dirt road.

Bianca felt her legs go numb. She grabbed the edge of the counter. She was just about to take a seat when a series of bizarre sounds popped from outside in the bullpen.

*CRACK! CRACK! CRACK!* All around the bullpen, every computer monitor in the office glowed brightly and then SNAPPED off.

"What the fuck?" Jim spun around, looking at the monitors.

"Power surge?" Arnie asked as a matter of explanation.

Jim looked up at the fluorescent ceiling lights that remained on. "Could be. Is it just the monitors?"

Charlotte's fingers flew across her keyboard typing different commands to get some sort of reaction. The monitors remained dead. "Seems to be."

"It's not just communications. All the security monitors are down too," Arnie observed. "We're blind on the holding cells. External security monitors too."

Charlotte hopped up and navigated her way across the bullpen to the CPU closet. She pulled open the door. Inside, the rack of CPUs were all dead.

Charlotte hit the rack and pulled a few interconnecting cables. "You little bitches. For real? All of you?"

———

Like the gentle sound of waves rhythmically hissing against the sand, Ray's whispered words repeated themselves over and over in the dark silence. "Ne... suan...nunn...me..." His body slowly rocked back and forth hypnotically as he perched on the edge of his cot. Behind him, the shadows in the dark corner began to coalesce into something dense. A small child's voice broke Ray's chanting rhythm.

"It found us."

Ray's eyes snapped open. He spun on his cot.

The little seven year old boy stepped into the pale light. His torn shirt pulled off his shoulder. His tattered shorts covered with dirt and his pale little legs were scraped and bruised. There was a worried look in his large, haunted eyes.

A tearful smile burst onto Ray's face. He leapt up, rushed to his son and gathered him in his arms. He clung tightly to the boy as he gushed with relief. "Oh Danny. Thank god you're here." The boy hugged his father back and they remained that way for a long moment, neither of them wanting to let go. "I wasn't sure where you went... I... I thought I lost you," Ray continued with a growing tremble in his voice.

"I've been here, Daddy. You just weren't looking."

Ray pulled back from his son, addressing him at arm's length. "Look, I think there's another way to fix this. That police woman knows it. I just need to get her to listen to me... With her help, maybe we can figure a way to—"

"It's too late."

"But we need to at least try," Ray desperately pleaded.

A distant look settled on the boy's face. "Daddy, this is the only way... you know it is."

Ray searched his son's little face, grasping for any way to delay the inevitable. "But... but even if it is, I'm stuck in here and they've taken it from me. I don't know where it is."

"I'll take care of that," the little boy assured him.

Ray struggled with the truth of their situation, his momentary feelings of hope slipping away.

"We don't have a choice. We have to do it." Danny's plain words sounded far beyond his years. It was a sad, grown up acceptance he'd had no choice in having to make.

Ray pulled his son to him tightly. Tears welled in his eyes. Tears of longing and sadness for what had happened so many years ago to his son. Why him? Why did it have to happen to such an innocent and loving child. Ray took an unsteady breath, his voice cracked with pain. "I... I'm going to miss you, Danny. God, I'm going to miss you."

"Me too Daddy,... me too."

A powerful jolt of adrenaline shot through Ray. His eyes snapped open. He bolted awake on his cot with his heart pounding. He looked around at the cell in the dim fluorescent light and slowly sat up. He took a cleansing breath to shake off his nightmare.

*Nightmare. Was it really?*

Nightmares and reality had been collapsing together for Ray so much that it was hard to tell which was which. Was he even awake now? He rubbed his eyes and stood up unsteadily. And then he stopped cold.

His cell door was standing open.

Ray stared at the impossible sight for a moment, trying to make sense of it all. He had to still be dreaming. Ray stepped across the cell, reached out and touched the open door frame. The glossy painted metal was cold on his fingertips. He slipped the frame into his palm and squeezed tight. This was real. The door was open.

Ray took a final look back at his empty cell and then slipped out the door. Danny had done just what he promised he would do and now it was Ray's turn to live up to his promise.

————

*Focus... focus... I'm in charge.*

Bianca was in fight mode. She snapped the circuit breakers back and forth one at a time in the rear hallway as Jim stood behind her. "It doesn't make sense. It's got to be something in this circuit breaker box." Everything else seemed to be working. The lights were on. The building was definitely getting electricity. She finished snapping the last breaker. "Anything?"

"Nothing!" Charlotte yelled from the bullpen.

"Shit."

Bianca turned and started back into the bullpen. Jim followed. The adrenaline had taken care of her headache. She had absolute clarity in moments like this. Get the monitors working again. Never mind what had happened to it or why. She stepped up to the CPU closet where Charlotte was poking around. "Let me look."

Charlotte stepped aside. Bianca crouched down. "Is there an incoming power line in here?"

"Yeah. Two of them all the way in the back there," Charlotte answered.

Bianca crawled into the cramped closet, pushed aside the cascading bundles of wires and squeezed between the CPU racks.

Jim was over at the bank of monitors, futilely punching and re-punching the power buttons. Arnie came up with an extension cord he had plugged in in the back hallway. "Let me get over there." Jim moved out of his way. Arnie found a power cable from one of the monitors and plugged it into the extension cord.

*CRACK!*

The monitor suddenly flashed on with a burst of static. In that brief second, Jim thought he saw something on the screen. But what he saw didn't make sense. It was a dense, black human-like form in

the center of the pale electrostatic energy. "What the fuck is—"
The image went black.

*CRACK!*

Sparks surged through the CPU closet, searing the wires.

"Bianca!" Charlotte dived down, grabbed Bianca and pulled her out just as the entire closet burst into flames.

"Watch out!" Arnie raced over with an extinguisher, yanked the pin and blasted the flames with the plume of white powdery mist.

Jim ran up to Bianca and Charlotte. "Are you okay?"

Charlotte coughed and nodded. Bianca wiped the powder off her shirt. "I'm okay. I'm fine."

Arnie emptied the last of the extinguisher into the closet. The flames were out.

"What the hell did you guys do?" Bianca demanded.

"Nothing. I just tried plugging a monitor directly into the wall," Arnie explained.

"That wouldn't change anything in the CPU closet," Charlotte assured them.

Bianca looked over at the smoldering closet. Her clarity of purpose was suddenly getting very murky. She needed to re-focus on the big picture. "Alright look, we're not going to have these security monitors up anytime soon. Someone should go down and check in on the holding cells."

"I'm on it!" Arnie started off to the stairs.

Bianca coughed, futilely waved the powdery smoke. "And let's get some windows open. We have to get this smoke out of here."

"They're locked. I'll do it." Charlotte hurried to her desk and yanked open the top drawer. She took out a glass jar filled with keys. The old station had a million odd things that needed keys— cabinets, drawers, screen doors, random padlocks. Nothing important. The important keys were kept with the Watch Commander, which was Bianca tonight. The keys in the jar were for things that they left unlocked so they never really needed them. But the windows were different. They were just always locked. No one in the high desert ever opened windows. It was either too hot or too cold. Charlotte sifted through the glass jar, found the one she was looking for and hurried to a window. She twisted the key in the lock and pushed outward. It thudded to a stop about six inches open when it hit the heavy mesh security screen that was welded on the outside.

"That's as far as they go?" Bianca asked.

"Afraid so."

"Just get as many open as you can!"

———

Arnie strode down the basement hallway in full cop mode to the holding cell doors. As he stepped past the partial entryway wall, the row of cells at the far end of the room came into view—

Ray's cell door was open.

"Shit." Arnie clawed for his pistol, spun around in a panic. No sign of Ray. He hurried over to the open cell and stepped inside. He ducked low, looking under the cot. Nothing. He started to turn back when something caught his eye and he looked up—

The drunk prisoner's body was hanging in the adjacent cell by his shirt that was twisted around his neck. "Mother... fu..." Arnie clawed for his radio.

*WHOOSH! CLANG!*

Arnie spun around—The cell door had slammed shut.

He raced over and yanked on the door. It was locked tight. His trembling fingers fumbled with the radio, trying to find the transmit key. It suddenly squelched loudly, then started to buzz. Smoke swirled out of it, followed by a burst of yellow flame. Arnie cried out and dropped the hot radio. It clattered to the floor as the smoldering plastic started to melt. "...The fuck?"

And then he heard it. Softly behind him. The voice of a thirteen year old boy. A voice he had not heard in many years. "I did it for you, Arnie."

In that instant, the sound of his younger brother's voice collapsed the thirty years that had transpired since the last time he saw him alive.

It was late September on a cool fall evening back in Easton, Massachusetts. A small working class town not known for much these days, but if you asked a local, they'd proudly tell you they were known for the shovels they forged to build the transcontinental railway. There was so much iron in the soil that the Town River was a dark rust color. Arnie had been raised there by his mother when his father left them shortly after Arnie's younger brother Justin had been born. As typical, Arnie had been thrust into the role of "man" of the family. But unlike the cliché, Arnie never took the reins and stepped up. He resented his little brother for constantly looking up to him and he resented Justin for causing his parents to divorce. Things only got worse when Arnie grew older, especially the year he was a senior in High School. That was the year when it all came crashing down. That early Fall evening.

Arnie was waiting in the family car as he looked down at his watch, frustrated. It was already 4:30. What was taking him so long?

"Justin! Come on. You don't want to be late!" The truth was, Arnie didn't want to be late for Linda. She had finally said she'd go to the next level with him and he wasn't about to mess this up. Telling his mom that he'd go watch Justin play football was the only way he could get the car for the night.

Arnie tapped the horn. The screen door on the small single story house banged open and Justin came rushing out in uniform, carrying his football helmet. "Sorry! Sorry! Coming!"

Arnie checked his face in the rearview. The acne on his chin had gotten better, thank God. Hopefully Linda wouldn't notice his outbreak on his neck. Justin hopped into the passenger seat and Arnie pulled out. They cruised out onto Central Street, to the Junior High School.

"Make sure you watch when I go to the far end right before the snap. That means we're doing my buttonhook play."

Arnie checked his watch. It was 4:45. Linda had told her parents she was going to study at a friend's house at 5:00. Arnie was going to meet her outside Dunkin' Donuts at 5:15. There should be enough time to find a seat in the bleachers, wave to Justin and then get the hell out of there when the game started.

"Did you hear me?"

"Yeah, yeah. Buttonhook. You're on the end."

"But don't tell anybody because if they see me going to the end, then they'll know."

Who the fuck was he going to tell? Spies in the bleachers? No one gives a shit about Junior High football. They're all a bunch of little kids. Arnie could never figure out why Justin was always worrying about stupid things like that. What's the big deal? Things like school, football and girls always seemed to fall into place for Arnie and tonight wasn't going to be an exception. He had had his eye on Linda ever since she was a freshman. That first dance where he saw her in her low-cut jeans with her perfect tight ass. And those tits. Damn. That's when he knew it was only a matter of time. And he had been right; the last couple dates had gone well, but tonight it was going to the next level. No more hand jobs. Tonight she was going down. It was a done deal.

"Thanks, Arnie."

"Huh?" Arnie snapped back to the present.

"Thanks for coming tonight. First game and all. What was it like for you?"

"What?"

"When you started?"

Really? Who the hell knows. Arnie had a hit of weed before the game. It seemed like any other game. "It was tha bomb," he was used to conjuring up the right response to get his little brother to shut up.

Justin smiled. "I bet."

Arnie pulled into a space in the Junior High parking lot and shut off the engine. "Come on."

They hopped out and joined the group of parents and students walking to the field. Arnie checked his watch again. Just enough time.

"I'll look for you," Justin promised.

"Yeah. I might be up in the back. It looks crowded."

Justin waved and ran off toward his teammates.

It was the last time Arnie would see him on his own two feet.

As promised, when the buttonhook play was called, Justin glanced up into the bleachers. He didn't see Arnie, but he didn't have time to search everywhere. The stands were pretty full like Arnie had said. Justin was pumped. Everything was happening so fast. This was it.

The ball snapped. He went deep and button-hooked back around. And that's when it happened. He felt a brittle *CRACK* from somewhere deep in his body when he was struck from behind. His feet were swept out from under him and he hit the ground with a bone crushing thud. A searing pain washed over him.

And then blackness.

Arnie's mother had to work the night of the game so she had let Arnie take the car so he could attend. She was cleaning her last room at the motel when the manager appeared at the door. His face was drawn and white. She shut off the vacuum cleaner. She couldn't remember the words he spoke. All she remembered was the shock and pain she felt when he told her. She immediately tried to call Arnie but got no answer on his cell phone. The manager drove her to the hospital and that's when she saw her baby lying there in bed. Tubes and wires. Trachea in his neck. The steady sound of the ventilator pumping. There was no life left. No warm smile to give her every morning. No giggles or laughter. No hugs. Nothing.

Arnie returned to the school with a smile on his face around nine o'clock that night. He had gotten what he wanted. Linda had performed like a pro and he was well sated. He went to the field only to find it deserted. He tracked down the grounds keeper and found out the game had been called after "the accident."

It would take another month until Arnie's mother could gain the courage to pull the plug. That month was hell for Arnie. The silence from his mother was greater than any words that could be used to punish him. It wasn't his fault, but somehow it was. It was always his fault.

And now there Justin was, standing outside the closed cell door in his blood-covered football uniform. A trachea tube was sticking out of his neck and his back was twisted grotesquely where it had been broken.

Arnie stumbled back, recoiling from the grisly sight.

"I didn't see you," Justin gurgled. "It wasn't for nothing, was it? You were there?"

"Jus... tin," Arnie whispered dryly.

"Just once... Just one time I wanted you to be proud of me."

Arnie's back slammed up against the cell bars. He closed his eyes tightly, trying to wipe the horrific image away, his heart thundering in his chest. A strange, brittle metallic sound echoed through the dark cell from behind him. Arnie opened his eyes and spun around. Two of the vertical solid steel bars were bent wide apart. The white enamel paint was cracked and flaked away.

*What the fuck?*

Arnie looked closer at the impossible sight. The opening almost seemed wide enough for him to squeeze through. He slowly reached out, testing with his fingers to see if the bent steel was real. It was.

He looked back into the cell. His brother was gone. Arnie took a cleansing breath, then tentatively extended his arm between the bent bars, then withdrew it and looked back at the opening. The bars remained the same. Arnie's mind began to race. He couldn't explain what had bent them open, just like he couldn't explain how his dead brother had appeared in the cell. None of that mattered now. He looked over at the wall just outside the cell. The red Lockdown alarm button seemed close enough. He could lean through this opening and hit it. That would bring help.

Arnie took a shaky breath, then leaned forward, stretching his arm toward the alarm. He came up short. He took another breath, then leaned further, this time moving his shoulder all the way through. His fingers grazed the alarm button. He pushed further still, leaning halfway through the opening...

And that's when the brittle metallic sound began again.

Arnie looked over his shoulder in a panic. The bars were straightening out by some unseen force.

*Fuck!*

Arnie lurched backward, but the bars gripped his torso. He screamed in agony as he felt the cold steel bars dig deeper and deeper against his spine as they straightened out. He knew there was no way out. He was going to die.

In a final blind panic, he jammed his fingers against the alarm button. At the very same instant, the steel bar snapped his spine in two with a sickening *CRACK!*

Just like Justin's back had been broken all those years ago.

# CHAPTER SEVEN

The shrill alarm echoed throughout the station. In the first floor office bullpen, the heavy steel security doors rumbled down on the front and back door with a loud *CLANG!* The alarm had triggered a complete building lockdown. Charlotte looked at the flashing alarm panel above her station. "It was triggered in the holding cells!"

Bianca and Jim drew their pistols and hurried toward the stairs. Charlotte snatched up the land line— *BLEEP! BLEEP! BLEEP!* The disconnect signal blared from the receiver. "What the fuck?"

Jim and Bianca had just reached the stairwell, when—

*BOOM!* A bright white flash lit up the mesh metal security windows from outside. All the lights in the building flickered briefly and died, plunging the entire station into darkness.

The alarm stopped.

And then there was nothing.

Just darkness and silence.

Bianca groped for the small flashlight on her belt and clicked it on. "What the fuck happened out there?"

Jim stumbled his way over to the window and squinted out through a narrow crack in the security mesh. "I... I think it's the power pole... yeah, looks like the transformer on the power pole blew."

"Hey guys!" Charlotte called over to Bianca and Jim.

Bianca shined her flashlight across the dark room to Charlotte, who was holding up her cellphone. "Land lines are down. And so is my cell."

"Your cell too?" Bianca asked in disbelief, and then immediately checked hers. Sure enough, her screen read: "No signal."

Jim checked his. Same thing. "The cell relay must have been on that power pole out there," he ventured.

"Why the hell isn't the back-up genny coming on?"

There was a moment of silent confusion. Bianca's mind began to race: It could be a diversion for a potential escape attempt. It could be an assault on the station. Or it could be just random bad luck. No matter what it was, it didn't change the basic fact that the station was vulnerable without power. There was not enough Xanax left in her system now to fight the adrenaline. She sprang into action.

She rushed to the weapons storage cabinet and unlocked it with her master key. Inside were several semi-automatic AK style rifles. They had been recent acquisitions because of the world they lived in these days. She pulled out two. "Jim!"

He looked over at her and she tossed him one of the rifles.

"Charlotte!" She tossed the other one to Charlotte, then reached back into the cabinet and grabbed three ammunition magazines. She pulled down a rifle for herself, then locked the cabinet again.

"Here!" She tossed Jim a mag. He caught it and slammed it into his rifle. She tossed the other to Charlotte, who examined it and gingerly snapped it into place.

"Check the back door. Make sure we're secure," Bianca ordered.

Jim clicked on his flashlight and headed over to the back hallway. He paused at the entrance, shined his light down the empty hall, then continued onward. He reached the heavy steel emergency shield that covered the outside door. He tested the handle. It was locked solid in place. Jim had seen this dust-covered emergency shield poised above the door for years and wondered if it really did anything. Part of him was surprised it had actually worked given the general condition of the old building. But it had. Perfectly. They were now sealed in the building. Nothing could get in... or out.

Back in the bullpen, Bianca checked the handle on the security shield that covered the front door. It too was locked tight. She moved to the front window and peered out through the steel mesh. Smoke was still swirling from the large transformer on the pole and the power lines were scorched. In the far distance, she could see the headlights of the cars passing back and forth along Highway 29 as if nothing unusual had occurred. Clearly, no one had noticed the explosion. Why would they? Most of them barely knew the police station was even back here. It was the way things worked out here in the high desert. Live your life and mind your own business.

Bianca looked away from the window when Jim returned from the back hallway. "We need to get down to the holding cells." Bianca knew the only way she could get through this was to prioritize the problems and tackle them one at a time. The alarm had been triggered in the holding cells, most likely by Arnie. They needed to get down there and find out what happened. She could tackle the next problem once she had more information.

Bianca crossed the bullpen to the stairwell entrance and paused. She lowered her voice to a whisper and pointed. "I'll take left. Jim cover right. Charlotte behind us."

Bianca and Jim took up positions on either side of the stairwell. "Clip 'em up." Jim and Bianca clipped their flashlights onto the barrels of their rifles. They aimed down the stairwell, scanning their beams of light along the walls. It was empty all the way to the first landing.

Charlotte tentatively came up behind them fumbling with the flashlight until she could get it into place. "Shouldn't I stay up here?"

Bianca looked back at the uncertain woman. She knew

Charlotte had specialized in communications and never thought she'd be in a situation like this, but she had gone through the academy and she was trained. Bianca was facing a big unknown down in the basement and needed all the back-up she could get. "Let's just get things cleared down there, then you can come back up."

Charlotte took a shaky breath and nodded. "Sure, okay right."

Bianca looked back at Jim and whispered, "Ready?"

Jim nodded. Bianca pressed her back against the left wall in the stairwell and slid inside. Jim slid in opposite her on the right wall. Charlotte took a final look behind her at the bullpen, then pressed against the wall and slid in behind Jim. Bianca nodded and they all started down the steps, keeping their rifles with their flashlight beams aimed ahead of them. Their pace was slow and deliberate. One quiet step at a time. Closer and closer to the unknown.

Try as she might, Bianca couldn't help her mind from racing again. She was flooded with possible scenarios of what they might find down there. Was Arnie in trouble? Had the prisoner somehow managed to escape? Was the prisoner waiting to ambush them? Or maybe it wasn't Arnie who had triggered the alarm. And if it wasn't him, who had? Bianca took a shallow breath.

*Stop. Stop. Stop. Don't get ahead of yourself.*

She had to stick with what she knew, but she had to be ready for anything.

They reached the first landing and Bianca held up her hand. They stopped. She steadied her breathing, then looked at Jim. He nodded in understanding. Their training had kicked in perfectly. They both raised their rifle barrels up. She gave him a nod and they whipped around the corner in unison, aiming down the next flight of stairs.

It was empty too.

They proceeded downward as carefully as they had before, one step at a time until they made it to the bottom of the stairwell.

They both panned their barrel flashlights through the basement hallway that stretched out in front of them.

It was empty.

Bianca exchanged a quizzical look with Jim, then looked back at the hallway. "Arnie?!" Bianca's voice reverberated into the darkness.

They waited for a reply.

Nothing. Just the dead silence of the stifling subterranean hallway.

Bianca took a moment to weigh her options. The next stretch down the hall would be more risky. If someone was going to ambush them, they'd be exposed. She looked back up the stairwell behind them— Off to one side she saw a double door with vents on the top. There was a yellow industrial symbol stenciled on the dingy doors indicating high electrical current.

The generator room.

Bianca made eye contact with Jim. He had seen it too. "Come on," she whispered. They retreated over to the generator room doors. Any possible place someone could hide had to be cleared before they went further. If not, they'd be leaving themselves vulnerable to an ambush from behind. Jim stepped back, leveled his rifle at the door. Bianca stepped to one side, reached over to the handle. She silently counted, "One, two, three."

Bianca flung open the door with a bang. Jim whipped his barrel flashlight across the old generator in the small room.

Empty.

Jim eased off his aim. Bianca took a step toward the old generator, and then it hit her— A foul, rotten stench.

Bianca coughed. Charlotte covered her nose and mouth. "What the fuck is that?"

Bianca covered her mouth with her elbow and looked closer at the base of the old generator. A pool of black oil and what looked like rotting blood and bile oozed out from the generator's tank.

"No wonder it didn't kick on," Jim observed. "Looks like that oil hasn't been changed in years."

"Oil? That's not like any motherfuckin' oil I've ever seen," Charlotte coughed.

Bianca kneeled. Charlotte was right. Something was very off. Several flies buzzed around the lumpy, putrid ooze.

Everything about tonight was getting more and more strange. Hearing Henrick Whitfield's name after all these years. The monitors going down. The alarm. The transformer blowing. And now this. Bianca couldn't help but try to connect everything. It was human nature. Conspiracy theorists did it all the time.

*Stop. Breathe.*

She had to remind herself that sometimes things happen that have nothing to do with each other. Coincidence is just coincidence.

"We have to keep moving," Jim urged.

His words snapped Bianca back to the task at hand. He was right. She stood up and closed the doors. Of all the things that they needed to deal with, this was the least pressing.

Bianca turned back to the hallway and slid up against the left wall. Jim assumed his position along the right wall. Charlotte stepped in behind him. Bianca gave them both a look and nodded.

They started down the long hall, stepping lightly on the glossy linoleum to avoid any unnecessary sounds. Bianca and Jim slowly scanned their barrel flashlights back and forth through the darkness ahead. Charlotte kept an eye on their backs.

They finally reached the entrance to the holding cells— Another one of the heavy security doors had slammed down over it, sealing it tight. Bianca exchanged a look with Jim. He gave her a reassuring nod, then quietly set his rifle down and pulled the flashlight off the barrel. He crossed over to a metal plate on the wall next to the far side of the door that read: "Manual Over-ride." He started loosening the thumb screws that secured the panel to the wall.

Bianca looked over at Charlotte. "Keep us covered."

Charlotte nodded and turned her back to them, scanning both ends of the dark hallway with her rifle at the ready. Bianca stepped up to the security door and pressed her head against it. The cold steel felt good on her overheated ear. She covered her open ear and the hallway sounds plunged into muffled silence. There was only her heart thumping and her shallow breathing. She held her breath and listened carefully for any possible sounds inside. There was nothing.

She finally leaned back and pounded her fist three times against the steel. "Arnie?!" She pressed her ear once more to the door and listened for a response.

Nothing.

Jim finished with the last thumb screw and pulled the over-ride panel off the wall. Inside was a heavy geared crank that was covered in a pale red coat of dust; it was obvious it hadn't been used in a very long time, if at all. He held his flashlight with one hand and gripped the crank with the other. He gave it a tug. It didn't budge. He set his flashlight down. "Give me some light here."

Bianca unclipped her flashlight then stepped up behind him and shined her beam onto the over-ride crank. Jim put both his hands together on the crank and gave it a forceful yank, trying to turn it counter clockwise. Nothing. He took a deep breath and tried again, straining against the stubborn crank. It didn't budge. "Motherfucker," Jim swore angrily.

Bianca sighed, frustrated, and pounded once more on the door. "Arnie?! Anybody! Can you hear me in there?" Her loud voice echoed in the empty hall. She leaned against the door again, listening.

Still nothing.

"Maybe it's just too damned thick to hear anything through it," Charlotte theorized.

"Or maybe no one's in there anymore... at least no one alive," Bianca said grimly. Charlotte took a moment to consider this disturbing possibility. The thought weighed heavily on Jim too.

Bianca felt there was no reason to sugarcoat any of this with them; they all had to be clear-headed about what they could be up against. She knew Arnie would not have triggered the alarm and locked himself in if the prisoner had escaped before he arrived. But it was possible Arnie could have been overpowered by the prisoner, then triggered the alarm after the prisoner escaped. That scenario would mean Arnie was now unconscious in there, or dead, and the prisoner was on the loose inside the station. "We have to sweep the entire station. If the prisoner somehow managed to escape, he's locked in here with us now."

Jim nodded, grabbed up his rifle and clipped his flashlight back in place. Bianca clipped her flashlight back too.

"Let's finish down here and then work our way back upstairs all the way to the second floor. If he's loose, he could've slipped past the bullpen when the power first went down." Bianca gave them both a look. "Ready?"

Jim and Charlotte silently nodded back at her. Bianca turned, and was about to start deeper down the hallway, when they heard it—

*Tap... Tap... Tap...*

It was slow and hollow, echoing from the other side of the security door.

# CHAPTER EIGHT

Everyone froze and looked over at the heavy door. They were all questioning the same thing: Did they really just hear that? They remained motionless, listening. And then—

*Tap... Tap... Tap...*

It happened again. Slow and deliberate.

"Shit!" Bianca hurried back over to the door and yelled, "Arnie?!" She pressed her ear once more to the steel.

*Tap... Tap... Tap...*

Bianca looked over at Jim and Charlotte. "He's alive in there." She pounded her fist against the door. "Arnie! Are you okay?"

She waited for a reply. This time there was no response.

Charlotte joined Bianca at the door with a worried look on her face. "Something's not right."

Jim set his rifle down and hurried to the over-ride crank. "We've got to get this fucking door open!" Jim gritted his teeth and pulled desperately on the crank with his newfound adrenaline. No use. It remained frozen tight.

"Arnie! Hold on! We're going to get you out of there!" Bianca yelled at the security door. She anxiously looked up and down the empty hallway for something to help Jim. She finally considered the rifle she was holding. It might work. She yanked the clip out of the rifle, ratcheted the chamber to make sure it was empty. "Here." She held the rifle out to Jim.

He grabbed it, turned it over, and started pounding on the stuck lever with the butt of the rifle. The old metal vibrated with each hit, causing the powdery rust to swirl up in a reddish cloud. Encouraged by this seeming success, Jim raised the butt higher and struck harder and harder until finally—

*Clunk!*

The old crank jogged loose.

Jim gave Bianca a victorious smile, tossed the rifle back to her and grabbed the crank with both hands. He grimaced and pulled with everything he had.

*Click... Click... Click...*

The lever started to turn slowly. The heavy old door groaned and began to rise.

Bianca looked back at Charlotte, who was eagerly watching their efforts. "We got this, Charlotte. Just watch our backs." Charlotte nodded and looked back at the dark hallway.

Bianca dropped to her knees and shined her flashlight through the sliver of darkness that was forming at the bottom of the door. "Arnie!" She yelled into the narrow opening.

Jim paused to catch his breath and listened. There was no response.

"Keep going!" Bianca ordered.

"Wait." Jim panted, lowering his voice to a whisper. "What if it isn't Arnie?

He was right. For all they knew it could be the prisoner who had tapped for help. He could be waiting in there to ambush them. Bianca's anxious mind raced to evaluate their options, but finally came to the conclusion that it was a chance they'd have to take if Arnie was alive and in trouble. She pressed her face against the cold linoleum floor and peered through the gap. Her flashlight beam swept across the partial entryway wall which was a few feet away on the other side. "I don't see anyone," she whispered. "Go slow."

Jim resumed his efforts and the door continued to slowly rise. Bianca retrieved her rifle and snapped the ammo cartridge back in place, then re-attached the barrel flashlight. She dropped back to the floor, pulled her rifle up next to her and scanned the barrel flashlight beam underneath.

The resistance in the crank began to increase. Jim bore down harder, but his strength was waning. "It's starting to freeze up again," he panted heavily. He gave a final yank, but the stubborn lever wouldn't budge any further. He stepped back and examined his progress. He had managed to get the heavy door a little over a foot off the floor.

Bianca scooted to the end of the door and panned her barrel flashlight off the edge of the partial entryway wall on the other side. Her beam stabbed deep into the dark holding cell area, but the angle wasn't enough to see the cells on the other side. "Arnie! Arnie, are you okay?!" She called out, then listened carefully into the darkness. There was nothing.

Jim dropped to the floor next to her. "I can fit under there."

Bianca eyed the gap under the door and agreed. "Yeah, I'm with you."

Jim slid up parallel to the bottom of the heavy door, then reached back and grabbed his rifle. Bianca stopped him. "Wait on the other side until I get through. We'll go to the cells together."

Jim nodded, then exhaled and twisted his torso so his head went first under the door.

Bianca watched Jim slowly pull himself underneath until his feet disappeared into the darkness. She gave a final look back at Charlotte. "Hang tight."

Charlotte took a shaky breath, clutching her rifle. "Yeah."

Bianca started pulling herself through the gap.

On the other side, Jim climbed to his feet and pressed against the partial entryway wall with his rifle at the ready. He looked down at Bianca, who was about halfway through, then he turned and slid to the edge of the wall. He swung his rifle around the edge. His barrel flashlight beam panned through to the shadowy maze of cell bars in the distance. He saw a dark form on the ground in Ray's cell at the far end. "Arnie!"

At the same instant, the heavy security door behind him groaned loudly. Jim spun back around. The massive door shuddered violently and lurched downward several inches—

"Bianca!" He tossed his gun aside and raced to Bianca, who was still under the door.

In the hallway, Charlotte ran to the lever and gripped it with both hands. The door shuddered again. "Get out of there!" She screamed.

*CLACK CLACK CLACK...*

The heavy door ratcheted downward, threatening to cut Bianca in half. Charlotte tried to resist as hard as she could, but it was no use. The crank broke free from her grip and spun.

Inside, Jim yanked Bianca through the gap just before the massive door slammed shut, sealing them both inside.

Charlotte pounded on the door in a panic. "Are you guys okay in there?!"

Jim helped Bianca to her feet. They could hear Charlotte's muffled voice from outside in the hall. "Bianca! Jim!"

"We're okay!" Jim called back.

Charlotte pulled on the stubborn lever, but it remained frozen. "I can't move it! It's jammed!"

Bianca called back to Charlotte, "Okay! Okay, don't worry. We'll find another way out!"

Jim gave Bianca a look. "What other way? This is a fucking holding cell."

Of course he was right, but that wasn't the point. Bianca knew what Charlotte needed to hear. The insecure woman was suddenly all alone out there, and she'd be their only line of defense against the prisoner if he was on the loose. She needed some assurance.

But Charlotte was already well aware of her new dangerous predicament. She gripped her rifle tightly, keeping careful watch on the hallway. Her mouth was bone dry as her throat tightened. "What?... What should I do?"

Bianca could hear the fear in Charlotte's trembling voice, so she answered as calmly as she could. "Just... just stand by for now."

Jim turned his attention back to the dark cells beyond the partial wall. "I saw something over there." Bianca stepped up beside him. They both turned the corner and started toward the cells, carefully scanning their barrel flashlights for any sign of an ambush. They reached Ray's cell on the end and both swung their barrels to the floor inside. Their lights illuminated Arnie's crumpled body.

"Arnie!" Bianca pushed the cell door. It swung open. She hurried inside and dropped to Arnie's side. She checked for a pulse and listened for breathing. There was nothing.

Jim stepped in behind her, scanning his barrel light around to the cell next door. He stopped at the bloated blue face of the drunk prisoner, hanging from his twisted shirt. "Bianca!"

She looked up and saw what he was aiming at. "Jesus Christ." She snatched up her rifle and went to Jim's side. Things had suddenly become clear. "That crazy motherfucker who did this is out there with Charlotte someplace." They exchanged a look of understanding, then Bianca hurried back to the heavy security door and yelled, "Charlotte!"

Outside in the hallway, Charlotte snapped her attention to the door. "I'm here! I'm here!"

"We need to find a way to radio out for help," Bianca's muffled voice said from the other side. "The squad cars outside. They should be working. See if you can override one of the security doors and get out there to one of them."

*Override a security door? Really?*

Charlotte took a moment to get her head around this. Things must be bad in there. After all, Jim had barely managed to get this one open. Charlotte swallowed dryly. "Well... I... I can try," was the best she could summon up.

"Good. You should have copies of the squad car keys in your desk."

"Yeah. I do," Charlotte confirmed. She took a shallow breath and looked back at the dark hallway. She was alone in this now. She took a moment to gather her courage, then asked the question she really didn't want to know the answer to. "Is... is the prisoner in there too?"

There was an uncomfortable delay, then Bianca's voice finally responded, "No. No, he's... he's not."

*Jesus fucking Christ.*

Charlotte felt her legs go weak. She braced herself against the door.

"Come back and let us know once you've radioed out."

Charlotte closed her eyes; she could feel her heartbeat throbbing in her neck. "Okay... yeah, I will." Charlotte opened her eyes again and steadied herself. This wasn't supposed to be her life. None of it was. The last thing she wanted to be was a cop like her father. She was always the pretty one. The popular one. The one that was going to live the fairytale life. She cursed her decision to join the force when her modeling dreams in L.A. didn't pan out. She should have done something else. Anything else. But when your father is high up in the Riverside P.D. and he tells you that he can set you up with a desk career, you do what makes sense to do at the time. And now here she was in Hell, facing a killer on the loose in a sealed building.

*Fuck.*

Charlotte pressed her rifle stock up against her shoulder and stared down the barrel. She carefully panned the light in both directions down the dark hallway, then started back to the staircase. She moved slowly, deliberately swinging her rifle back and forth. If the prisoner was going to attack, it could only be from one of those two directions.

She reached the bottom of the staircase and paused with her back to the corner. Now it was going to get harder. She leaned out and aimed her rifle up the stairwell. The shadows from the hand railing stretched and shifted as she panned her light up to the landing. It was empty. Charlotte slowly climbed the first set of stairs, constantly looking behind and ahead of herself. When she reached the landing, she paused in the corner again. She panned her light up the final flight of steps to the office entrance. All clear. She continued onward, one slow step at a time until she finally reached the entrance to the office bullpen.

She stopped again, panning her barrel beam across the dark offices. There were a million places someone could lie in wait up here. Under desks, behind filing cabinets, beyond cubicles. Her single beam of light couldn't possibly expose them all. This next stretch over to her desk to get the keys would have to be an act of faith.

Charlotte stepped out of the stairwell and slowly made her way into the office bullpen. Her heart was racing now as she slowly circled around in 360 degrees, her barrel light beam stabbing through the jumble of shadows. She pressed onward, past the burned out CPU closet, and finally arrived at her desk in the communications center cubicle. She shifted the rifle over to her left hand and reached to her belt with her right. Her shaking fingers unclipped her key ring. She quickly took her eyes off her surroundings and looked down at the keys. She separated her desk key and opened her top drawer. She looked back at the dark office again, not wanting to let her guard down. She took a shallow breath and then looked down again at her drawer...

*Thump.*

Charlotte's eyes shot back up at the dark office.

*What the fuck was that?*

She whipped her rifle up, gripping the weapon with both hands as she aimed in the direction of the sound which had come from somewhere off in the distance near the back hall. She slowly moved the barrel to the left and then back to the right. There was nothing there. Charlotte steadied herself. She was in control here. She had the rifle. She swallowed dryly, then raised her voice. "Show yourself!"

She waited, keeping her rifle aimed across the dark bullpen, then tried again. "There's no way out of here! Come out with your hands high!"

Charlotte surprised herself by how in control she sounded, but she also felt like she was playing a part in some cop movie. She straightened herself and stood her ground. Listening. Watching. The moment stretched in time. It was deathly still.

*It had to have been someone, right?*

Or maybe it wasn't. Maybe a breeze from outside had shut a door somewhere upstairs. After all, the windows were still pushed open against the security mesh covers down here. Charlotte tried to slow her racing thoughts. No matter what it was, it didn't change what she had to do. She shot another look down at her open drawer and grabbed the glass cup of keys. She set it on her desk, fished out a set of back door keys and copies of the squad car keys. She stuffed them in her pocket, then slowly, carefully started away toward the back hallway.

As the glow from her barrel light receded across the bullpen, the darkness returned. But it wasn't an empty darkness. A dense shape slowly grew from the shadows, stretching taller and coalescing into the ominous black human-like form.

It was here and it was following her.

# CHAPTER NINE

**B**ianca aimed her barrel flashlight up at a ventilation grate in the ceiling outside the cells. "What do you think?"

"Worth a try," Jim said as he set his rifle down. He crossed into Ray's old cell, grabbed the cot and dragged it out under the grate. He climbed up on it and gave the grate a tug. It was screwed tight into the ceiling. He carefully examined the screws, then reached into his pocket and fished out some change. He took a quarter and tried to fit the edge into the screw slot. It was too thick. He pulled out a dime and did the same; it fit. Jim pressed the dime hard into the slot and gave it a turn. It moved. He gave Bianca a grim smile and turned it again. It was working, but it was also painfully clear that it was going to take a long time to get the grate off.

———

Upstairs by the back security door, Charlotte clenched her flashlight in her teeth as she quietly pulled the override panel off the wall. She looked over her shoulder down the hallway to the dark office bullpen— It was still and silent. She took the flashlight out of her mouth and shined it onto the override crank. It was in much better shape than the one in the basement; there was none of the rust they had encountered down there. "This might work," she admitted to herself. She set the flashlight down, gripped the lever and gave it a tug. She was right. It slowly turned.

Charlotte gave another look behind her, then leaned into the effort, using her body weight to turn the crank counter-clockwise. The heavy security door slowly began to rise. A simultaneous sense of relief and panic swept over her; on one hand she could see her freedom slowly emerging in front of her, but on the other hand she was vulnerable with her back to the offices. She doubled down, cranking as fast as she could. The door was now almost two feet above the floor. It would need to be much higher. She wouldn't be able to slip under it like Jim and Bianca had because the regular back door was on the other side and it was locked and...

*Someone's behind you.*

Charlotte recoiled from the crank and spun around in a panic, grabbing up her rifle as she went. She shifted the rifle to her right shoulder and snatched up the flashlight. She panned the beam across the empty office bullpen down the hallway. There was nothing there.

*No. No, that was real.*

She couldn't ignore what she had felt. Someone had just been standing behind her. She was sure of it.

But where were they now? How could they be gone so fast? Charlotte's heart thundered in her chest as she scrutinized the empty hall and offices beyond. Her mind struggled to focus through the fog of panic. Doubt began to creep up on her certainty; after everything she had been through tonight, maybe she can't trust her instincts anymore. She was a total mess, that was obvious. Who's to say that couldn't make her feel things that weren't real.

"Fuck, girl... get your shit together," she heard herself whisper.

Charlotte finally turned back to the override crank. She redoubled her efforts and the door rose up just above the doorknob. She stopped, caught her breath and reached for the key. She slid it into the knob, gave it a twist and the back door sprung open. The cool night breeze swirled inside.

Charlotte crouched down, picked up her rifle and slowly panned the barrel light through the open door. She could see from the garbage dumpsters to the left of her all the way to the far right end of the fence. It was clear. She ducked under the door, then stood up outside. She paused and listened. She could hear the distant wash of cars passing by on the far-off highway and the shrill oscillating sound of a nearby cricket. She slid along the back of the station to the corner and peered around. Her barrel beam swept across the line of squad cars parked along the side of the building.

Charlotte took a cleansing breath, then darted toward the nearest squad car. Her barrel beam bounced wildly around in front of her as she ran. When she reached the trunk, she stopped and steadied her aim. Her beam illuminated the back of someone seated in the driver's side. Charlotte hesitated, trying to make sense of what she was looking at. And then it hit her—

"Ben?"

He didn't move. Puzzled, Charlotte hurried around the side of the squad car. Maybe he couldn't hear her through the closed windows. "Ben?!" She tried again, louder.

Still nothing. As she grew closer she could see that something was very wrong. His head was oddly tilted to one side. He was motionless. She grabbed the door and yanked it open. Ben's body slumped outward, then jerked to a stop, still constricted by the seatbelt. His face was pale gray. Coagulated blood oozed from the corner of his blue lips.

Charlotte stifled a scream. She spun around in a panic, scanning her barrel light behind her. The parking lot was empty. Her breathing became shallow and fast; the world was spinning around her. She locked eyes on the next squad car. It was empty.

She bolted over, pulling the car keys from her pocket. "Oh God... oh God... oh God," she hyperventilated as she searched for the right key. She finally found one that matched the "YV- 03" stenciled on the roof of the car. She plunged the key in the door and threw it open. She jumped behind the wheel, shut the door, and slammed down the door locks.

Her rapid breathing was all she could hear in the silence as she slipped the keys in the ignition and gave it a turn. The engine chugged and skittered, then suddenly roared to life. The radio crackled and squelched with normal police activity.

*Thank God.*

Charlotte took a deep breath, then snatched up the radio handset and squeezed it tightly. "San Bernardino, this is Yucca Valley Station. We have a 10-24 in progress. Code 3. Code 3. Officer down. Repeat. Officer down. Request immediate assistance!"

Charlotte released her death grip on the handset and listened.

Nothing. Just dead static air.

Charlotte sighed anxiously, "Come on... come on." She tuned the radio to an All Channel Emergency frequency, then squeezed the handset and tried again. "This is Yucca Valley Station seeking all-points assistance! I have a 10-24 in progress. Code 3. Officer down. Repeat. Officer down!"

Charlotte released the handset button again and waited.

Nothing.

"Shit!" She anxiously pressed the handset button once more. "This is Yucca—"

"Yucca Valley Station, come in." The voice on the other end was low, faint and filled with static.

Charlotte felt a rush of relief as she turned up the volume and clenched the handset once more. "Yes! Yes, this is Yucca Valley Station. I have a 10-24 in progress. Officer down. Code 3."

She leaned toward the radio speaker, listening carefully to the roar. After a moment, her relief began to fade. What the Hell was going on? She jammed down the handset button, irritated. "Do you copy? I said I have a 10-24 in progress. Officer down. The prisoner we were holding escaped. He... He killed at least two officers. Our power is out. We need immediate assistance! We need armed—"

"Yucca Valley Station... you're dead." The faint, menacing voice proclaimed through the wash of static.

Charlotte hesitated. What did he just say? Her mind flip-flopped back and forth, trying to make sense of this. Did she not understand him? Or did he say what she thought he said? She slowly pressed the transmit button. " This is Yucca Valley Station. I... I'm not reading you clearly. Please repeat." She released and waited. There was nothing more. Just the static. Charlotte reached over and adjusted the frequency on the radio. "This is Yucca Valley police station seeking an all-points call for emergency assistance. I have—"

"Charlotte."

Charlotte froze at the sound of her name. Her eyes locked on the radio. She remained motionless, not sure what to do. After a moment, she slowly squeezed the handset again. "Who is this?" She waited as the static filled the air, then tried again. "Identify yourself."

There was a long moment, and then the low, static-filled voice spoke again. "It's over, Charlotte."

Charlotte went flush; she began to tremble. "Who?... Who is this?... How do you know my name?"

The static grew louder, filling the car. It began to close in on Charlotte. She could feel it strangely reach into her ears and slide down her throat. It was alive.

"There's no place to go Charlotte. No escape."

The presence within her began to pull now, taking her breath from her lungs. Everything she felt within her body melted away. It enveloped her. It was inside her. She was it, and it was her...

"All you have left to do, Charlotte, is exactly what I tell you to do."

———

Jim's fingers ached as he pinched the dime and turned the screw in the grate. He pulled his hand down and shook it. "Jesus, my fingers."

"Want me to take over?" Bianca asked from below as she held the flashlight.

"Let me at least get this one," he said as he put the dime back into the stubborn screw slot. He could only twist it a half-turn at a time before he had to take it out and reposition his hand back again. It was slow-going and frustrating. He struggled with it in silence for a moment, then glanced down at her. "You know, I... I wasn't trying to give you shit earlier... about not calling me."

*Oh come on, not this. Not now.*

Bianca searched for a response and finally decided all she could do was ignore him. Maybe he'd take the hint and drop it.

"It's just that... I guess I expected a little more honesty from you."

No such luck. "Really, Jim? You're going to do this now? Just do us both a favor and leave it alone, alright?"

"A little late for that, don't you think?"

"No. No, I don't"

"Well I do. I know you didn't go home after work last night."

"So now you're checking up on me?"

"Just worried when I didn't hear from you, that's all."

Bianca realized he wasn't going to stop. She would have to plead for mercy. "What do you want from me? I told you it was never going to be more with us than it was."

"Right. And I get that. But I guess I didn't know I was going to be lied to."

"That's bullshit, Jim. I was honest upfront about how it was. I told you not to get involved if you couldn't handle it."

Jim turned his attention back to the stubborn screw in the grate. He gave a couple more turns, then muttered, "Right."

Bianca watched him wrestle with the screw; she could see his frustration building. She knew this wasn't over.

Sure enough, Jim didn't disappoint. "You know... No matter how much you beat yourself up for not being there for your niece, it won't change anything."

*You motherfucker. How dare you bring her up.*

"Shut the fuck up, Jim. Don't ever go down that road with me. Ever!"

Jim blanched at her visceral anger. He knew he was playing with fire when he said it, but he didn't think she would go off on him like that. In his mind, he wasn't just saying it to punish her; he really believed that on some level things could be different between them if she could see what he saw.

"Well," he finally said quietly. "Just know that if you ever decide to forgive yourself, try to do it while there's still someone around who gives a shit about you."

Jim finished taking out the screw and tossed it aside. He dug his fingers under the edge of the grate and gave a tug. Half of the grate dropped open.

"Here." Bianca handed him the flashlight. Jim aimed it up into the partially open ventilation shaft. There were steel bars blocking the opening beyond.

"Shit." Jim reached in and tugged on the bars. They were welded solidly in place. "They're not going anywhere." He climbed down off the cot and wiped the sweat from his brow. "Any other ideas?"

Bianca looked around the holding cells in despair. "I guess we just have to hope that Charlotte got a call out for—"

*CLUNK!* The loud sound came from outside the heavy security door across the room. Jim and Bianca exchanged a look. They grabbed their rifles and hurried around the partial entryway wall.

"Charlotte?! Is that you?" Bianca called out. They reached the door and stopped. There was no answer. "Charlotte?"

They waited for a response, and then—

*CLANK! CLANK! CLANK!* The heavy steel door began to rise on its own.

# CHAPTER TEN

"**B**ack! Back! Back!" Bianca waved Jim away from the door. They took up defensive positions on the other side of the entryway wall, rifles aimed at the rising gap. The heavy steel door continued to rise slowly until it finally stopped about five feet off the floor.

"Charlotte?" Jim called out.

There was no reply. Bianca exchanged a look with Jim. He had barely been able to get the door open a couple of feet. How could Charlotte have done this?

Jim reached up and turned off his barrel flashlight. Bianca gave him a puzzled look. What the hell was he doing? He raised his finger to his lips, signaling her to be quiet, then crept to the edge of the door. Bianca kept her rifle aimed at the gap. The crazy motherfucker was taking a stupid chance, but she honestly couldn't think of another option.

Jim slowly crouched down and peered under the security door. The hallway outside was dark, but it was empty. He quietly reached up and turned his barrel light back on. He panned it under the door. The beam swept back and forth in the hallway. There was no one there. Jim paused a moment, then looked back at Bianca. He pointed to himself and then over at the opening.

*No no no... don't!*

Bianca angrily shook her head, but Jim waved her off. He ducked under the door and went out.

"Jim!" Bianca whispered angrily. Goddamn him. The prisoner had probably opened the door and this was a trap. "Jim!" She whispered again, her panic rising.

Jim finally appeared once more under the security door. "It's clear."

Bianca sighed, then braced herself. This was no time to let her guard down. She kept her rifle aimed and ready as she stepped up to the door and ducked underneath.

Jim waited for her with his back against the wall outside. Bianca swept her barrel up and down the empty hallway. "He's fucking with us."

"Could be... but we're out now, and that's a whole lot better than before."

"We've got to find Charlotte." Bianca turned to leave.

"Wait." Jim stopped her. "He just opened this. He couldn't be far."

*Thump.* A low sound echoed from down the hall in the direction of the evidence room. Jim and Bianca spun around just in time to see—

A shadowy figure duck around the corner.

—————

Charlotte sat behind the wheel of the squad car with the engine at an idle. She gazed out the windshield at the closed parking lot gate several yards in front of her. The low rumble of the powerful engine filled her ears. A far away thought tried to get her attention: Why was she doing this? But then the thought drifted away again, just like it had before when she pulled the car up here. Everything seemed like she was a spectator. She was aware what she was making her body do, but couldn't understand why.

And she liked it. She felt peaceful and powerful.

She felt her foot slowly rise off the brake and hover over the gas pedal. Her foot floated there a moment, then suddenly thrust downward. The powerful car lurched forward with a roar. She saw the gate rush toward her in the headlights. The explosion of twisted steel sounded far away as she felt her face softly come to rest against the airbag.

A warm smile curled her lips and she closed her eyes. She felt herself drift away again. She remained there, not wanting to leave the blissful place she had found. But then another thought swept over her. Her eyes snapped open. She pushed the airbag out of the way and opened the crumpled door.

The squad car was firmly enmeshed in the gate, creating the perfect barrier. No one could get in or out of the parking lot now. Charlotte climbed out of the driver's door and into the swirling steam and smoke that poured from the buckled hood.

She paused for a moment, admiring her work. There was a small glowing fire somewhere deep in the twisted gleaming steel. Sparks flickered through the haze like fireflies on a warm summer night. It was quite beautiful, she decided.

But she had work to do. She reached down to a gas can by her feet. She had a vague memory of siphoning the gas from Ben's squad car earlier. The taste of gasoline was still in her mouth.

She picked up the can and strolled back to the remaining two squad cars. Ben's body was still hanging out the open door. What a beautiful garden she had planted, Charlotte thought, and then she began watering her flowers with the gas can.

The fuel splashed over Ben's body and then across the hood as she moved to the car next to it. She emptied the can and tossed it aside, then reached into her pocket and took out a flare.

This will be glorious, Charlotte assured herself as she twisted off the cap and struck the flare. The bright red flame glowed in her eyes. She gave a final look at her newly found garden and then tossed the flare.

It bounced on the hood and rolled, igniting the gas as it went. The flames roared to life, spreading quickly across the car and down to the ground, then over to Ben's body in the other car.

Charlotte felt the comforting warmth of the raging flames as they engulfed both squad cars. In the orange flickering light, she could see her reflection for a moment in the windshield. She smiled. She was happy that she wasn't alone.

Her new companion was right there by her side.

Bianca and Jim crept silently down the hallway, keeping their backs against the wall and their rifles at the ready. Their barrel flashlights were off to avoid announcing their approach. Neither had spoken a word since they saw the shadowy figure duck away. They had been communicating with looks and gestures. As they approached the corner in the hall that led to the evidence room, they began to hear the distant sound of jingling keys.

Bianca paused at the corner and carefully peered around. The evidence room door was ajar. It was dark inside. She ducked back around the corner and then mouthed the words, "it's open." She signaled for them to continue and they turned the corner together.

Bianca slipped up next to the open door with Jim right behind her. She kept her rifle poised, ready to draw down as she peered through the crack. She could barely make out the rows of storage shelves in the darkness as she tried to focus on the direction of the jingling sound. It seemed to be coming from the far end of the room.

Bianca looked back at Jim, pointed and nodded. She reached to the door and slowly pulled it open. They gave each other a look, and then slipped inside.

*What am I doing here?*

Charlotte was lost, trying to remember how she had gotten to her desk in the dark office bullpen. It was like she had just awoken from a deep sleep. She was here for some reason. It seemed to have something to do with Bianca. But what was it? And why was it so dark in here?

And then a soft voice whispered to her, "Charlotte."

Charlotte spun around. A slender silhouette approached, stepping into the dim glow by her desk. It was the shell of a young woman; she was nothing but pallid skin stretched over bones. Her stringy hair hung in patches on her bald scalp. The worst outcome from the ravages of anorexia.

"What about now, Charlotte? How do I look now?"

Charlotte stared at the ghastly sight, stunned. This can't be happening. It was impossible that she would be looking at her childhood friend again. Not like this. She was dead. Long dead.

Charlotte closed her eyes and took a steady breath.

*No no no… it's not real.*

Charlotte remained in the blackness with her eyes closed. She thought she was finally past all this. But here it was again. The pangs of guilt came flooding in as her mind raced back to the day everything between her and Wanda changed forever. A time in her life she struggled for years to come to terms with.

It was a hot October Saturday afternoon at Charlotte's home in Riverside. She lived in one of the best houses in the endless housing tracts that filled the flat, smoggy community. The lawn was impeccably mowed and the flower beds were tilled to perfection. The police force had given Charlotte's father a comfortable living and he wanted the world to know.

That Saturday, Charlotte was floating on a blow-up raft in the pool with her eyes closed. She heard the sliding back door open. She looked up and saw Wanda tentatively step outside in her one-piece black bathing suit. "I... I don't know, Charlotte."

Charlotte sat up on the raft and took a moment to evaluate her self-conscious friend. So what if her legs were a bit thick and she still had a belly that sagged? Wanda had been through a lot and she needed to hear something positive. "I think you look great." And Charlotte meant it. At least she did at that moment.

Ever since they first met in grade school, Wanda had always been a bit bigger. As kids they never gave it a second thought. They loved playing video games, talking Harry Potter, and hanging out. It wasn't until middle-school when hormones kicked in that things got harder for Wanda. "One Ton Wanda" was the chant that had brought her to private tears on many occasions. She got good at pushing it out of her mind and playing it off, but her real cure was to eat her way through the anxiety. A cycle of pleasure and pain that was comforting in its predictability.

Charlotte lived in a very different world. She was always slender and she blossomed into the kind of young tween that beauty magazines loved. She was asked to the Junior High school dance. She was asked to be on the cheer squad. She was asked to run for class president and even considered it briefly but decided she was busy enough with her many extra-curriculars. Still, Wanda and Charlotte remained friends and occasionally got together and played their video games. But by eighth grade, Charlotte began to feel a restlessness when she hung out with Wanda. She had other friends by that time that talked about boys and Wanda seemed so different.

By the time high-school came around, they had gone their separate ways. They always remained friendly in the halls, but it never went beyond that. Charlotte was in with a set of successful friends that played their parts perfectly. Wanda struggled to make friends. Charlotte continued to witness other kids occasionally teasing Wanda. But she made a point of pretending she didn't see it, and she never joined in the jokes that were made behind Wanda's back.

It was the summer before senior year when things changed for Wanda. She had spent the summer on a weight watcher's program and when she showed up at school, it was hard to recognize her. Charlotte was even stunned. Over the next few months, they began to reconnect a bit more over things they seemed to have in common like difficult classes and comparing cute boys. Until there they were once again, together at the pool. The day it all took a horrible turn between them.

"You know, you should try a two-piece," Charlotte suggested.

"Really?" Wanda asked dubiously. She knew she had lost a lot of weight, but she still had a way to go before she looked like Charlotte. Not that it was a competition... Or was it? Wanda shook off the negative thoughts. She had something she was bursting to tell Charlotte. She couldn't wait to hear what Charlotte was going to say.

"Yeah. They have some with high cut bottoms, you know. In case you want a little support on your thighs."

It rolled off Charlotte's tongue so effortlessly. Did she mean her thighs were still too thick? Wanda took a moment and buried the insecure thought. She wouldn't let this little dig get in the way of her big news. "Yeah. Maybe I'll try that."

Wanda picked up her can of Diet Coke and crossed to the lounge at the edge of the pool. She took a seat. "You know Derick White, right?"

Charlotte was taken by surprise. Why would Wanda be talking about Derick White? She finally looked over at Wanda, bewildered. "Of course. Yeah."

"He... he talked to me on Friday. He was... he was nice."

Charlotte felt her face flush. Derick White? Really? Is she saying she thinks Derick might like her? She's out of her fucking mind.

Derick was a long distance runner on the track team... And he was gorgeous. Charlotte had an all-consuming lust for Derick. All her raging hormones were focused on that one perfect boy. Charlotte had talked to her friends about him. But they all told her she had to play it cool. Charlotte was the prize. She wasn't the one who could approach him. He had to approach her. After endless discussions with her friends and seemingly endless tortured nights pining for him, Charlotte decided she had to take the first step. She let a friend of Derick's know that she "kind of liked him."

But now this?

Charlotte blurted out an involuntary laugh. "You and Derick? Seriously?"

Wanda was taken aback. Why was that funny? And then it came rushing back like a tidal flood. All of her anxiety and insecurity. "Well, I... I don't know. He just, you know... whatever. He came up to me." Wanda stammered, withering beneath the avalanche of feelings.

It was at that moment when Charlotte realized she would have to destroy Wanda. There was absolutely no way "One Ton Wanda" would get the guy she so desperately craved, especially after she had already told her friends.

Sure enough, Charlotte made good on her threat. She started with her friends, at first referring to Wanda as "the whale waiting to get out of the chubby body." She even revived the One Ton Wanda joke.

It wasn't long before Charlotte's cruelty got back to Wanda. And Wanda was crushed. She expected the teasing from others but not Charlotte. Why would she do it? And the spiral began. Wanda's desperate eating produced the exact result she hated. It's hard to imagine how much words can hurt. But when your entire world is the school, there is no escape. Older people forget that those years are a time in life when we are so vulnerable and so cruel to each other.

Charlotte eventually did go out with Derick. The build-up was tremendous. The gossip spread quickly through the school about the impending hook up. But after an awkward attempt to seduce him in the Applebee's parking lot ended with Derick unable to get hard, Charlotte turned on him too. Gay, she decided. Anyway, what did it really matter? There were plenty of others lining up for her.

After graduation, Wanda went down a path of self-destruction. Eating and binging. Trying to get some control over her life that always seemed so desperately out of control. After many torturous years and failed attempts to change, she finally died in the hospital with her parents at her side.

Charlotte was in LA when she heard the news. She had been struggling herself with her attempts at modeling. In LA, she wasn't the stand-out beauty she was at home. The competition in Hollywood was overwhelming and heartbreaking. Hearing about Wanda created a perfect storm and Charlotte plunged into a deep cycle of regret, guilt, and self-pity. She finally returned home and slowly pulled herself out of it. The job her father got her helped a lot, and for the past several years she was feeling back to her normal self...

Until now.

There she was. Standing before Charlotte in all her distorted hideousness.

"I know I'll never be pretty like you, but you can't call me fat anymore, can you? Not now. Not the way I am now."

# CHAPTER ELEVEN

Jim lead the way through the dark evidence room, creeping silently toward the sounds with his rifle at the ready. Bianca brought up the rear, occasionally glancing back over her shoulder. They passed by row after row of evidence shelves until they finally discovered the source of the jingling.

It was Ray.

He was at the far end of the row, frantically searching through Arnie's key ring trying to find which one would unlock the evidence cage where his backpack was stored.

Jim immediately drew down on him. "Freeze where you are!"

"Keep your hands where we can see them!" Bianca added.

But Ray took a sudden dive behind the far rack. Bianca and Jim both opened fire. Their bullets clanged and ricocheted off the metal racks. Jim darted down the row after him. Bianca cut down the next row over.

Jim rounded the far end of the rack and Ray leapt out, body slamming him violently against the rack. Jim lunged back at the frantic man, pinning him against the opposite rack. Ray groped for Jim's holster.

Bianca popped up behind them. "Freeze!" But there was no clear shot. Jim and Ray were tangled together in the darkness. Bianca advanced, keeping her aim true. Ray suddenly wrestled away from Jim, brandishing Jim's pistol. He opened fire. Bianca took a dive. The bullet thwacked into the rack, inches away from her. She quickly recovered, took up position, and returned fire.

But Ray was already gone.

Bianca jumped up and raced over to Jim, who was covered with blood from his broken nose. "Go! Just go! I'm okay!" he yelled as he waved her away. Bianca nodded and took off as Jim struggled to his feet.

Bianca burst out of the evidence room and into the hall. She heard Ray's rapidly retreating footsteps around the corner. She sprinted after him. Jim staggered out of the evidence room and followed.

Bianca rounded the corner and caught a glimpse of Ray ducking into the stairwell beyond the holding cells. She took aim.

Too late.

"Shit!" She raced down the long hall to the bottom of the stairs and paused. She expertly panned her barrel flashlight up the staircase. There was no sign of Ray.

Jim joined her, catching his breath and holding his bloody nose. "Up there?"

"Yeah. Come on." They started up the staircase.

They reached the landing and paused, panning their barrel flashlights up the next flight. It was clear. They pressed onward, finally reaching the entrance to the office.

They swung their lights into the bullpen...

Charlotte was sitting at her desk across the dark room with her back to them.

"Charlotte," Bianca whispered, relieved. But Charlotte didn't turn around. Bianca exchanged a curious look with Jim and tried again louder. "Charlotte!"

Still nothing from Charlotte. Bianca started toward her and Jim followed, carefully glancing behind them. As they grew closer they heard a rattling and clinking sound and they could see that Charlotte was busy doing something at her desk.

"The prisoner was in the evidence room. He came up here. Did you see anything?" Bianca asked.

Charlotte ignored her. Bianca finally stepped around in front of Charlotte and stopped cold—

Charlotte was furiously binge eating the keys from the glass jar and choking them down dry. Her lips were bloody from her torn up mouth.

"What the hell are you doing?!' Bianca cried out. She dropped her rifle and hurried toward Charlotte.

Jim peered through the metal mesh security window and saw the squad car tangled in the front gate and the other cars on fire. "Jesus Christ! All the cars are fucked up!"

Bianca grabbed Charlotte's arm, stopping her from stuffing another handful of keys into her mouth. Charlotte didn't react. She just stared off into space.

"Charlotte, can you hear me?"

Charlotte remained motionless... And then a flicker of her old-self surfaced. A terrified part of her that was still aware of what she was doing to herself begged, "Hel... help... me..." Tears welled up in her eyes and spilled down her cheeks.

Bianca opened Charlotte's fist and pulled the keys out. She reached for the glass jar...

*WHACK!*

Charlotte back-handed Bianca with a brutal, unnatural force. Bianca crashed into a cubicle and slumped to the ground, dazed.

"Hey!" Jim started toward her.

Charlotte smashed the glass jar on her desk. She grabbed the pile of glass and the rest of the keys and stuffed them all into her mouth. Blood spurted onto her desk.

Bianca rubbed the back of her aching head and looked over at Charlotte, dazed. "My God... Charlotte what are you?..."

Charlotte swallowed hard and coughed up a stream of blood. She reached for another pile of glass.

Jim grabbed Charlotte's hand. Charlotte swung around, clutching a long sliver of glass.

*SHUNK!*

Charlotte jammed the glass shard deep into Jim's throat above his Adam's apple. Jim's eyes went wide. He clutched his throat, trying to inhale.

"JIM!" Bianca screamed, as she struggled to her feet and raced to his side. He collapsed into her arms. His body spasmed. Bianca yanked the shard out of his neck and the blood sprayed everywhere. He gurgled and gasped.

"What the fuck did you do?!" Bianca screamed at Charlotte.

But Charlotte just calmly swallowed more of the glass and keys and then turned to Bianca. She spoke in a low, guttural, menacing voice. "Your niece, Taylor..."

Bianca froze at the sound of her niece's name.

"She was a very dirty little girl... just like the rest of them."

And then Charlotte reached up with a sliver of glass and slashed her own throat. She slumped forward onto her desk. Blood washed out from her severed carotid.

Bianca recoiled. At the same instant she felt Jim's body spasm in her arms. She looked down and saw his eyes riveted on her; he opened his mouth to speak, but nothing came out.

"Jim... Jim." She shook him, desperately trying to bring him back to her. But the light in his eyes began to dim.

"Jim..." Bianca's voice cracked. He spasmed once more and then she felt the full weight of his body in her arms as he went limp. His head lulled to one side; his eyes were now dull and lifeless.

He was gone.

Bianca stared down at him for a lost moment. Everything had happened so fast, it was too much to process. Nothing seemed real.

She finally lowered Jim's body and stood up. She looked in disbelief at the carnage surrounding her. The flickering glow from the smoldering squad cars outside the mesh windows illuminated the hellish scene. Blood dribbled from her arms; her clothes were soaked completely through. Her entire world had just crashed down around her.

*It's a dream. A nightmare.*

Her own mind tried to trick her into believing it wasn't real. But Bianca began to wrestle with her thoughts. She felt herself slowly drifting back until the reality of her situation finally snapped into sharp focus. She had to get out of the building.

Now.

If the gate was blocked, she would climb the fence. She'd take her chances on the razor wire on top. Anywhere would be safer right now than inside the station with the armed prisoner on the loose. She slowly picked up her rifle and backed away, then turned and hurried to the hallway.

She rushed to the back door where the security barrier was still halfway up. She tried the back door knob on the other side. It was locked. Bianca yanked out her master keys and sifted through them. She found what she was looking for, shoved it into the door lock, and gave it a twist. It clicked open. She grabbed the knob and was about to open it, when she heard—

Ragged guttural breathing coming from the other side.

Bianca froze.

She waited for a moment, listening. And then the ragged breathing stopped. She slowly pulled her hand off the knob then silently brought her rifle up to her shoulder and leveled it at the door.

"Back away from the door or I'll shoot!"

Bianca waited for a response. There was nothing.

*Now what?*

Bianca's mind began to race again. Should she just start blasting? Did her warning do the job? Who could be on the other side? She didn't have a choice. She had to go through; this was her only way out. Bianca swallowed dryly and reached for the doorknob again with her free hand, keeping the rifle trained on the door. She slowly pushed it open.

The door swung all the way open and bumped to a stop against the outside wall. She panned her barrel flashlight out into the dark parking lot.

There was no one there.

Bianca took a breath and gathered her courage. She stepped slowly through the doorway...

A flurry of gnashing teeth, putrid fur, and ragged claws suddenly rushed at her from the darkness. Bianca whipped her barrel flashlight wildly across the approaching menace. It was a pack of coyotes.

She reached out for the door and gave it a yank. It whipped closed, but the coyotes got there first. The door cracked into their necks. They yelped and recoiled. But several more took their place.

Bianca tossed her rifle aside and used both hands to pull on the door. The coyotes lunged harder. Bianca kicked at their snarling mouths, barely avoiding their razor sharp teeth. The pack behind them started clambering up over the others, doing everything they could to get to her.

The vicious animals were widening the gap. Bianca looked desperately around for some way to stop them.

The security barrier.

Bianca reached over with her foot and kicked the override lever. It started ratcheting downward. She waited until the last second, then let go of the outer door.

The heavy security barrier slammed down, crushing the advancing coyotes to death in a sickening splash of blood and pulverized flesh.

Bianca staggered back, catching her breath. She could hear the coyotes continue to yelp and snarl as they repeatedly slammed themselves against the outside door. What the fuck was this about? She had seen them become more aggressive earlier, but nothing like this. She couldn't risk going out there now.

She looked down the hall to the bullpen, then back at the stairwell. Her options were rapidly narrowing. She would have to hold up inside the station until morning when the dispatch from San Bernadino would arrive to pick up the prisoner. But where? Last time she saw the prisoner he was heading upstairs from the basement. He wasn't on this floor, so he had to be on the second floor. There was also still a chance he was just trying to escape, and if he was, who gives a shit? Going to the basement was her best option, Bianca decided. She could barricade herself in the evidence room. It was defendable. One way in and one way out.

Bianca took a deep, calming breath.

*Just hold it together.*

Bianca started down the hall. And that's when she heard it. A far off, sing-song little voice, "Biaaan... caaa..."

Bianca stopped dead. She waited. And then it happened again.

"Biaaan... caaa..." A child's voice. Faintly echoing from somewhere in the building.

# CHAPTER TWELVE

"Biaaan... caaa..."

It was wafting out of the stairwell. Bianca crept over, her rifle aimed dead ahead. She paused at the entrance, carefully panned her light down toward the basement, then up toward the second floor.

"Come out now! Keep your hands raised high!"

She waited.

Nothing. Bianca grew frustrated. She stepped onto the landing...

Rapid footsteps retreated on the stairs above her. Bianca whipped her barrel light upward. "Stop where you are!"

The footsteps fell silent. Bianca stepped cautiously up the stairs. "There's no way out! Come out now!"

*boom... boom... boom...*

An unearthly percussive pounding resonated from somewhere off in the bowels of the building. Bianca stopped in her tracks and looked down.

*boom... Boom... BOOM... BOOM...*

The banging sound grew louder as it came up the stairwell. Bianca took a step back. The banging was deafening now. The walls began to shake violently.

*WHAM!* The door slammed shut behind her. Bianca spun around in a panic, yanking on the knob. It was locked.

*CRACK! CRACK!* The walls splintered. The water pipes on the stairwell wall burst open. Scalding water gushed out; mixed with the cold, this caused a geyser of steam. Bianca dropped her rifle and shielded herself against the wall from the blast. She desperately yanked on the doorknob. The metal door frame began to twist and warp, permanently jamming the door shut.

And then the tremor fell silent.

The hiss of steam was all that Bianca could hear. She stepped back from the mutilated door.

*What the fuck was that?*

She had felt her share of earthquakes, but this was very different. It seemed as if it was coming toward her like it had a life of its own. The office door was sealed and going down was too risky; if there was another tremor, she could be buried. She picked up her rifle and looked upward. The staircase was obscured by the blasting steam that filled the stairwell. It was her only option.

She leveled her rifle and started up the stairs. Her barrel light could only stab through the swirling steam a few feet in front of her. As she neared the top landing, she saw a dark shadow retreat quickly through the mist. Bianca took aim. "Stop where you are!"

The shadow disappeared through the door to the second floor. Bianca lowered her aim and rushed up after it.

She stopped in the entrance to the second floor and panned her barrel light through the shadowy room. It was what they used as a lunch room and office storage. Jim had also cleared aside some of the old desks and filing cabinets and set up a make-shift gym using some old equipment that had been donated to the station a couple of years ago.

"This is your last chance to turn yourself in! Additional police officers will be here any minute!" Bianca paused to add emphasis to her lie, then added, "The building is sealed! There's no place for you to run!"

She let her words hang in the air for a moment. But there was no response. She finally took a step into the room, slowly passing the gym equipment and stacks of old filing cabinets.

A shadow moved behind her.

Bianca paused, sensing something, and then suddenly spun around. "Freeze!"

It was Ray. He recoiled and shielded his eyes from the blinding light.

"Don't move! Don't move or I'll shoot!" Bianca advanced on him, keeping her barrel aimed dead on. "Down on the ground!" Ray dropped to his knees. "Face down!" Ray laid face down. "Get your hands out where I can see them!" Ray reached outward. "Slow! Both hands out, palms down!" Ray slowly complied.

"Please... you have to help me," he pleaded.

"Shut up!"

"But we're both in danger."

"I said shut up! Keep your head down."

Ray lowered his head to the floor. Bianca felt her belt for handcuffs. She didn't have any. "Don't move. Just don't fucking move." She pressed her foot on his back. "How many others are there?"

"I... I don't know what you're—"

"Who's helping you escape?"

"No... no one."

Bianca leaned her weight into her foot. "Don't lie to me. Someone on the outside has been helping you. They blew the transformers."

Ray gasped in pain, "No... really there... there's no one helping me... I told you before who's doing all this."

Bianca pressed down harder. "Start giving me some real answers or this is going to get a whole lot worse for you."

Ray grimaced, gulping for air. "Okay... okay..." He was stuck; he realized he'd have to tell her everything he knew even if she wouldn't believe it. "This... this is all my fault... all of it... I was trying to fix it when you stopped me in the evidence room... We need to go down there and... and I can make it all stop."

"So there _is_ someone trying to help you?"

"No. Please, just... just hear me out... I know this doesn't make any sense to you, but no one's trying to help me... It's trying to kill me... to kill all of us."

"Why?"

"Because it doesn't want to go back."

"I told you to stop the bullshit. Who's down there? How did they get in here?"

"It's here because I did something... I did something I never should have done... and now... now I'm trying to fix it. If you help me, we can fix it."

Bianca stared down at the sweating, trembling man beneath her boot. What the hell was she doing? It was clear that he was out of his fucking mind and no matter how many times she tried to make sense of what he was saying it would never make sense. Bianca began to run her options through her mind again. At least she had a hostage now and if anyone else was here, she'd have some leverage. She'd have to find a way to permanently restrain him until morning. Bianca looked around the room for something that she could use as restraints.

And that's when it started again...

boom... Boom... BOOM... BOOM...

The unearthly hammering sound resonated up from the bowels of the building. Bianca looked around, startled. The walls around them began to shake. The gym equipment rattled; the dumbbells spilled to the floor. Stacked office chairs toppled over. The percussive pounding grew deafening. Bianca staggered back, shielding herself from the tumbling debris.

_What the fuck is all this?_

Ray cowered on the ground. He knew exactly what this was. He had tried to get her to help him but she hadn't listened. And now it was too late. It wasn't going to stop until they were both dead.

A large bookcase teetered above Ray; he rolled out of the way as it crashed down, just missing him. He looked over at Bianca, shielding herself beside a filing cabinet. The shadows in the stairwell door behind her began to shift...

The dense black human-like form emerged.

Ray panicked. It was here. "Behind you! Behind you!" He screamed desperately above the thundering noise.

Bianca felt a sudden icy burn on her ankle. Her first thought was that something heavy had fallen on her foot. But then the coldness began to sear her to the bone. She cried out in agony and turned to look but it was too late—

A powerful, unnatural force jerked her backward across the floor. She screamed and clawed at the carpet, trying to stop herself. Her shoulder brutally slammed against a fallen desk. She reached for the desk leg to stop herself but the force was too great. It continued to pull her and the desk until it crashed into the old metal lockers, crushing her hand. She cried out in agony and released the desk leg.

She was dragged into the stairwell doorway and then she suddenly stopped. Bianca looked around in a daze. The open stairwell door shuddered violently. Rotting blood and bile oozed from the hinges and ran down the door. Bianca struggled to make sense of the bizarre sight. And then, the heavy door violently swung loose on its own. Bianca was about to be crushed, when an office chair was shoved into the doorjamb at the last second. The door crashed against it, saving Bianca's life.

She looked up and saw Ray standing over her. He reached down, grabbed her by the collar and dragged her to safety inside the upstairs room just as the chair buckled and the door slammed shut with a deafening boom.

The tremor subsided. The unearthly percussive pounding receded once more down into the bowels of the building until there was...

Silence.

Bianca gasped in pain, clutching her wounded hand. She looked up at Ray with a lost look in her eyes. The world around her was suddenly something very different. If she hadn't just lived through it, she never would have believed it; there was no rational thought left in her mind to explain it. "Wha... what was that?"

Ray collected himself, catching his breath. He could see that she was finally ready to hear the truth. "The one who killed my son... and your niece," he answered.

Bianca looked up at him, bewildered; she knew what she was about to say made no sense, but she said it anyway. "No... no, we killed him... he's—"

"Dead. Was... Is." Ray reached down and helped ease Bianca back against a fallen cabinet. "Whatever drove Henrick Whitfield to do what he did was pure evil, and that kind of evil doesn't die. It lies in wait, probing each and every one of us, looking for a way out." Ray pulled a towel off a nearby gym rack and handed it to Bianca. "How is your hand?"

"My finger," she winced, "It might be broken." She carefully wiped the blood away and wrapped her fingers in the towel.

"Look, I knew I couldn't outrun the police. I came up here because I thought if anyone might believe me about all this, it would be you. You knew what kind of monster Henrick Whitfield was. I thought if I could just try to explain to you what I had done, there was a chance you'd help me fix it."

Bianca looked up at him, cradling her wounded hand. "And what exactly did you do?"

Ray looked away from her, struggling with his confession. "My son, Danny... after that monster killed him, my world collapsed. I was lost. My wife and I had nothing but pain between us."

Ray's mind began to slip back to that darkest of times; it was a place he so desperately wanted to forget, but never could. He remembered staring at Alison from a distance across their dark living room. The words between them had all been said. She gave him a silent final look and walked out the door, pulling her suitcase behind her.

Ray remained there in the darkness with the curtains closed. He couldn't tell day from night. It was only emptiness and silence. He stayed there for what could have been hours or even days; he had no way of telling.

And then he was done.

He felt himself slowly stand up. He silently crossed the living room, picked up the car keys from the entryway, and walked out the door. Ray drove the old family mini-van through the endless sprawl of the Inland Empire and out the 10 freeway into the low desert. The sun was rising over the dry, empty expanse as he headed east. He felt the heat of the scorching sun as it blasted him in the face. He didn't make a move to shield his eyes. It didn't matter.

He had just passed the Salton Sea, when he felt the engine chug and sputter. Finally, he thought, the car was out of gas. He steered to the edge of the freeway and rolled to a stop as the engine gasped its last breath.

Ray looked down at a bottle of water on the passenger seat, then back out at the rising sun. He finally opened the car door and stepped out, deliberately leaving the water behind.

The hot and dusty air filled his lungs as he walked across the uneven desert terrain. His scuffed dress shoes slipped unsteadily on the sand and rocks. If he fell, it wouldn't matter. Nothing mattered.

Time became unhinged again. The only sound was his breathing and the crunch of his footsteps. Eventually he stopped sweating. He could feel his heart pounding in his neck. His vision grew blurry. He was floating now. Finally free from the pain, the loss, the guilt. His legs gave out and he plunged downward into blackness.

The steady sound of dripping water punctuated the stillness when Ray finally opened his eyes again. He saw strands of long gray hair hanging over him. He focused past the hair to the face of an old woman in her late 70s. She gazed down at him as she dabbed his face with a wet cloth. She saw that he was awake but said nothing. After a moment she finished and silently walked away. Ray slowly sat up and looked around. He was inside a cave that had been adapted as a living space.

He had been found by a group of aging nudist hippies who referred to themselves simply as The Family. They had taken him to their commune along the rocky bluffs in the low desert. The encampment was a combination of rusting school buses and trucks parked near several caves in the bluffs that they had found. Most of the hippies were in their late 70s. Their skin was leathery and brown from all the years living as nudists in the desert.

At first, Ray felt like a stranger in a strange land. But as the days passed, he realized they were no different than he was. Over time he, too, began to remove his clothes; first his shirt, then shoes, then pants. Piece by piece, he set them aside until he was completely nude. There was never a lot of talk and no one ever asked him why he was found face down in the desert with no water or food. That was fine with Ray. It was liberating not having to explain anything about himself and his painful past.

Once a week, they all disappeared with no explanation and didn't return until the following morning. Ray didn't ask why and they didn't tell. He was happy spending his time in the community garden or carrying the buckets of water back from the well over the ridge. He knew everyone's faces and no one's name.

But even in this amorphous community, Ray began to see a hierarchy. The oldest woman, who had attended to him in the cave, and her two female partners were consulted on most decisions. All three had long, straw-like gray hair. They were all rail-thin and their breasts were long and narrow which swayed hypnotically as they walked. They spent most of their time inside the caves, weaving together odd pagan symbols made from bleached bird bones, human hair, and strands of leather that they would spend the day collecting.

Finally, as Ray huddled asleep under the blankets in the cave one cold night, he felt a gentle touch on his shoulder. He looked up and it was the oldest woman. She reached down and took his hand. Ray slowly stood and she led him out of the cave.

Outside, he saw the entire community moving out of the encampment. For the first time, they were taking Ray with them on their overnight venture.

They traveled single file up into the rocky ridge above the commune and then back down into a hidden box canyon. They silently took their places around a smooth rock outcropping in the middle of the clearing. The old woman took Ray to the rock and gestured for him to sit. She signaled to one of her partners and they came over, carrying the symbol they had made for him.

And then, for the first time, the old woman whispered in Ray's ear. "Debhuihka."

# CHAPTER THIRTEEN

**B**ianca stared at Ray in silence after he finished relating his strange story. "Debhuihka?"

Ray nodded. "It was a way to get what I wanted most."

Bianca looked down at her fractured hand and adjusted the cloth. There was nothing she could say. She didn't know what to believe anymore.

"Daddy?" A small voice suddenly called out to them from across the dark room.

Bianca looked up, startled, as she reached for her gun.

"No. No, it's okay," Ray assured her.

Bianca relaxed her grip on her gun. She stared in disbelief as a small figure approached them.

"Danny," Ray whispered, relieved, as the small boy emerged into the half-light.

"He'll be coming back. We have to go," the little boy said as he stopped in front of his father.

"Okay, honey. It's okay. We're going."

"What about her?" Danny asked.

"I think she understands now," Ray said as he looked back at Bianca. "Don't you?"

The truth was Bianca didn't know what to understand. There was nothing she could compare any of this to. "How is this happening?" She finally asked.

Ray studied Bianca's perplexed expression; it was clear she needed more. "Danny's death was... and always will be... tied to the monster who killed him. Their energy is forever connected. When I used the Dehibuika ritual and the symbol to bring him back, I opened a door and that allowed the monster to follow him."

"What does it want?"

"It exists only to consume life... to feed off it... it knows all of our deepest, darkest secrets... the things we feel the most guilty about... and it uses them to destroy us."

"Can it be stopped?"

"As long as I hold onto Danny, I hold onto his killer." Ray took an anxious breath and looked over at his son. "And the only way to send it back is to send Danny back."

"You can do that?"

Ray nodded. "By using the symbol that's locked up in the evidence room. I need it to perform the Dehibuika." Ray studied Bianca for a moment, gauging how his story was landing with her. "Look, I never would have brought Danny here if I had known that monster was going to follow him. Everything was so perfect at first when we got home together. I even called Alison and begged her to come back. I promised her everything was different." Ray hesitated, and then darkness clouded his face. "But by the time she returned, the monster had arrived. I knew I couldn't tell her what I had done." Ray trailed off into silence, struggling with the memory. "Before I... Before I could send them back, it... it killed Alison. And that's when I ran..." Ray swallowed dryly, choking back the pain, then looked at Bianca, pleading, "Please, this... this is all my fault. I accept that. I'm just begging you to help me fix it."

Bianca studied the tortured man for a moment. As strange as it all was, there seemed to be a logic to what he was saying. She also knew there was no point in denying any of it after what she had just been through. She finally broke the silence, "So then we have to get down there."

"Yes... Yes, thank you." Ray sighed, relieved. "But like I told you before, it will do anything it can to stop us from sending it back. It doesn't want to give up the power it found on this side of the divide."

———

Outside, the dark station was barely visible against the pitch black sky. The pack of coyotes swarmed around the back door, feverishly licking the rotting blood and bile that oozed out around the doorjamb. There was no infighting between them. There was plenty of the pungent excretion for all to devour.

The faint brittle sound of cracking rock caused the alpha male to pause. He stepped back from the door, looking warily at the ground beneath his paws. The others continued their feeding frenzy, unaware of his behavior.

*CRACK!*

The brittle sound was loud now, echoing through the night air. All the coyotes flinched and retreated from the door. The alpha's ears perked forward, focusing in on the sound that was growing louder and louder. Fissures began to form in the foundation of the building. The black bile and blood oozed out of the new cracks and spread out into the parking lot. The coyotes began to howl and yip anxiously at the phenomenon. And then...

boom... Boom... BOOM... BOOM!

The percussive pounding began to shake the ground beneath them. The coyotes flinched and lowered down onto their haunches to ride out the tremor.

———

Up inside the second floor room, the percussive tremors shook the building from below. Ray knelt by Bianca's side. "Can you walk?" Bianca looked up at the shaking gym equipment above her lost in her own world. "Officer?!" Ray shouted.

Bianca snapped out of her daze. "Yeah... yeah. I'm fine. It's just my hand." Bianca climbed to her feet, gingerly picked up her rifle with her good hand. "I'm Bianca. Just call me Bianca."

"Do you have keys to the evidence lockers?"

Bianca clutched the keys on her belt. "Yeah, I've got it. Right here."

"Okay then, we need to go."

Bianca followed Ray across the room to the sealed stairwell door. He looked back at Bianca and then tentatively reached for the doorknob. He gave it a turn. The door clicked open.

The percussive pounding filled their ears as Ray and Danny stepped into the dark, steamy stairwell. Bianca stepped up behind them and snapped on her barrel light. She swept the beam down toward the first floor landing. Ray gave Bianca a reassuring look and then started down. Ray and Danny's silhouette disappeared in the mist ahead of Bianca. She hesitated. Every instinct was screaming at her not to go toward the source of the sinister pounding. Her mind raced through any alternative and came up short. She was committed. She had to follow through.

She finally started down after them. Her boots slipped on the steamy, wet stairs and she steadied herself. She reached the first floor landing, where Ray and Danny were waiting. The percussive pounding began to intensify from the bowels of the building.

Danny looked up at his father, worried. "It... It knows we're coming."

Ray took Danny's hand and continued downward. "Hurry."

Bianca watched them disappear down into the misty steam in front of her. She started after them. Her boot slipped on the wet steps again, but this time she wasn't so lucky. She pitched sideways and tried to stop her fall with her wounded hand. It jammed into the railing and she cried out in agony.

The pounding grew louder, coming closer and closer up from below. The walls of the stairwell began to shake violently. Bianca painfully pushed herself upright. The railings in the stairwell began to vibrate. The concrete walls began to crack.

*BOOM! BOOM! BOOM!*

The pounding became deafening. Bianca froze in her tracks. Something was suddenly very different. The intensity was fierce. And then the seemingly impossible began to happen...

The entire stairwell below her started to twist closed like a throat constricting.

Bianca stumbled backward up the stairs. The steel hand railings and re-enforced concrete walls continued to crumble and twist in toward her, sealing her off from the basement below. She reached the second floor landing and dived into the room just as a railing ripped free and hurled toward her.

She felt a sharp pain as the metal cracked into her head.

And then darkness. Silence.

# CHAPTER FOURTEEN

The long, narrow hallway was lined with dingy yellow wall paper that was curled at the seams. The pink floral pattern was faded from the desert sun. The door to the bathroom at the far end of the hall was blown out from the light streaming inside. It was hot and dry in the old house. All that could be heard was the steady *drip... drip... drip...* of water splashing into some kind of deep pool.

Bianca tentatively pushed her way down the hall toward the bathroom door at the far end. As she grew closer, she could hear a little girl humming a simple and happy tune. Bianca squinted into the bright light as she grew closer to the door and an image began to form. It was Taylor, Bianca's niece; a petite, blond little girl. She was sitting at one end of a bath tub. She looked over at Bianca and smiled. "I waited and waited, but you never came."

Bianca stopped dead in her tracks. Taylor looked away and continued to hum her happy tune. Bianca swallowed dryly, then reached up and slowly pushed the door all the way open revealing an emaciated, hideous bald man outside the other end of the tub on his haunches. His angular knee bones and spine almost poked through his translucent, mottled gray skin. His shoulder and arm bones could be seen moving beneath his skin as he worked at something in the tub.

Bianca's heart began to race. The gray man sensed her watching. He stopped, then turned slowly and looked directly at her. "They're dirty... they're all so dirty." He raised his hand from inside the tub. He was holding a wash cloth, dripping in rotting blood and bile.

Bianca opened her mouth to scream, but nothing came out. She remained frozen, staring horrified at the ghastly image. And then out of nowhere, Bianca's sister leaned up next to her and whispered in her ear, "I hope you rot in Hell."

<hr>

That was it. The nightmare. Always the same. Over and over. Night after night. It was almost as bad as the real life nightmare Bianca lived through the day she forgot her niece.

That day had started with a jolt. Bianca had been working the nightshifts in San Bernadino. It was what rookies always got stuck with. She usually kept the curtain black-outs in her apartment bedroom closed until around two o'clock when her phone would alarm. But that afternoon her phone rang at twelve noon, jarring her out of her sleep. She groped for the phone on her nightstand and dragged it to her ear. "Yeah."

The voice on the other side was the watch Commander. "What time can you be here?"

Bianca struggled to focus her foggy mind. "Huh?... Uh... I..." She pulled the phone away from her ear and looked at the time. "It's twelve now. What's going on?"

"I've got an arrest in the meth case. You and Johnson pulled him over two nights ago. I want you in here to back up Johnson's account."

A jolt of adrenaline shot through Bianca. She never expected her routine nights patrolling as a rookie by Johnson's side would ever lead to anything but exhaustion and boredom. She sat up and swung her legs to the floor. "I'm on my way. Be there in half an hour."

Bianca hung up and hurried to the bathroom. She snapped on the light and grabbed her brush, then paused. Who cared if she didn't look perfect? This was her first chance to really be part of the team. She tossed the brush aside, put her hair in a pony tail, raced back to her room, and started putting on her uniform.

The next few hours went past in a blur. She made it to the station and went right into the interview room with Johnson. The interrogation became tense, but Bianca remained calm and backed up Johnson's account. By the time the suspect's lawyer arrived, they had gotten what they needed from him.

Afterward, she went with Johnson to the watch Commander's office and debriefed him on the interrogation. Johnson went out of his way to commend Bianca on her professionalism. They all shared a cup of coffee and continued to talk about life around the station. Bianca was on top of the world. She felt part of it all for the first time.

She was still riding her high when she reported in for her evening shift... And that's when her life came crashing down. She finally checked her phone for the first time, which had been left on silent during the interrogation. There were seventeen calls from her sister. Seventeen. It was a number Bianca never seemed to forget.

It was Thursday. Bianca had promised to pick up her niece after school before she had to report for her shift. With each message, her sister grew more frantic. Worry and concern gave way to tears and desperation. Bianca's entire world stopped as she listened.

Her niece had disappeared. Gone forever. No excuses for not picking her up could be offered. She had been swept up in her work and had forgotten. Her guilt overwhelmed her. She had felt so good about herself that day after the interrogation and all the while her niece had been waiting for her outside the school, alone and afraid.

Bianca's sister was inconsolable. She moved back in with their parents and spiraled deep into depression. Her only saving grace was her faith that had resurfaced. She clung to her Bible, constantly referring to it for guidance.

Bianca grew more and more distant from the family. It was too painful to visit but even more painful when she avoided them. She wanted to crawl out of her skin. Faith kept her sister from ever uttering words of blame, but it was always hanging over every interaction they had together.

Bianca had always been the ambitious one. She had made it through community college and then through the police academy. She prided herself on striving for a life beyond the lower middle class world her parents and sister seemed so content to live in. Bianca's ambition had begun to come off as selfishness. Always thinking of herself first, and her lapse that fateful day became part of the narrative.

Bianca soon found herself happy to comply with her new image. She began to stay out late, drink heavily, and take home stranger after stranger. In the mornings, she was able to spring back and be at work on time. She made sure that no one at the force saw who she had really become.

In the months that followed, more children were reported missing. Forensic evidence had been discovered that pointed to abductions. Bianca appealed directly to the lead detective team working the case, and with Johnson's help, she was accepted. She gave up drinking to focus on the case. The sleepless days and nights were welcome penance for Bianca. The very least she could do was punish herself with work. Her life only revolved around the case; she never let herself come up for air. And just when she thought her self-torture couldn't get any worse, they moved in on Henrick Whitfield's house that day and they discovered the bathroom and human remains. Her niece was among them.

It was a dark ending to a dark period of time. Bianca no longer had a case to obsess over and she started to drink again. This time, her alternative life seeped into her work life. There were off-handed comments and disapproving looks from coworkers. Bianca knew it was only a matter of time before she'd be counseled, so she took the job up in Yucca Valley.

And that was how Bianca found herself getting by, living day to day and drinking night to night. All until Ray Cutter had found her and her living nightmare came roaring back.

———

Bianca's eyes snapped open. She inhaled sharply. Her heart surged with adrenaline and she sat up. She squinted into the darkness, trying to orient herself. The toppled gym equipment and office furniture were a shadowy jumble around her. The faint sound of hissing steam could be heard coming from the stairwell.

She felt a hot throbbing sting on her forehead and she gently touched it. There was a gash from the railing that had struck her. She quickly pressed the towel that covered her wounded hand to her forehead to stop the bleeding. She tried to focus her thoughts, carefully going back over the moments before she was struck. The image of the stairwell constricting flashed in her mind.

*Did that really happen?*

Bianca had to check and see. She rallied her strength and pulled herself to her feet. Her head began to spin and she stumbled; she steadied herself by grabbing the edge of a fallen desk. She remained there, catching her breath.

*Gun... where's my gun?*

Bianca looked around at the rubble. She spotted her rifle over by the stairwell; she pushed herself off the desk and began to teeter slowly toward it.

*Thump.*

Bianca froze in her tracks. Her eyes snapped to a place across the room where the sound had come from. She squinted into the shadows. There was someone there; she could sense it.

Bianca turned and hobbled to her rifle. She snatched it up with her good hand.

"Bianca?" A small voice asked from across the room. Bianca spun around in a panic, groping for the flashlight on her barrel. "Bianca, is that you?" the little voice asked again.

Bianca snapped on her barrel light and scanned it across the room. The shadows stretched and moved as the beam passed the rubble, and then...

Bianca's little niece, Taylor, stepped out into the light. She wore her blue school uniform skirt and white shirt; her hair was neatly done in pigtails.

Bianca stared at the strange sight, stunned. Was she still dreaming? Was it real? "Taylor?" She finally whispered as she lowered the rifle.

Taylor slowly stepped toward Bianca; a winsome smile spread onto her little face. "You finally see me." Taylor reached out and gave Bianca a hug.

Bianca could feel her niece pressing against her. She set her rifle aside and slowly reached her good hand around and hugged Taylor back. The little girl's body was warm and Bianca could feel her slowly breathing in and out.

*It's her. It's really her.*

Tears welled in Bianca's eyes. "Oh God, Taylor. You're here." Bianca pulled the little girl closer to her.

"I followed him out of the darkness... that's when I saw you. I kept calling your name but you didn't see me."

"I see you now... I do now." The tears spilled over and ran down Bianca's cheeks. Every painful emotion that she'd been fighting to contain for the last few years came flooding out. It was like a dam had broken inside. Her body quaked as she began to cry. "Oh, God Taylor... I'm so sorry I forgot you there... Please forgive me... please..."

The little girl rested her head snuggly against Bianca. "It's okay, Auntie Bianca... I'm with you now... I'm here."

# CHAPTER FIFTEEN

Down in the basement, dust from the recent collapse in the stairwell hung in the air. Ray was covered in sweat as he pulled away pieces of the rubble and tossed them aside. His knuckles were raw and bleeding from the rough debris. He coughed on the dust. It was a desperate act that seemed almost futile, but he didn't know what else to do. He hoped that Bianca had survived and was upstairs on the other side of the collapse, but he had no way of knowing for sure.

"Officer! Can you hear me?!... Bianca?!" Ray called out, then paused, caught his breath and listened. There was no response.

"Daddy, we have to go."

Ray looked back at his little son, standing in the dusty hallway behind him. "I know, I know. Just... just let me get up to the first landing. Maybe she can hear me from there." Ray renewed his efforts.

"But we don't have time. We'll have to try without her," Danny pleaded.

Ray picked up his pace. The idea of opening the divide alone was daunting. Even if he could somehow get the symbol out of the evidence cage without Bianca's key, the monster was sure to be lying in wait. He would need her to watch his back when he evoked the Debhuihka.

Ray felt a hand suddenly land on his shoulder. He looked back once more at his son, who was pulling at him. "There's no time for this."

Ray could see the urgency in his son's face. He looked back up at the avalanche of debris and re-evaluated it through his son's anxious eyes. The boy was probably right. It was going to take hours to clear a way through the rubble, and even if he did, there was no assurance that Bianca had survived the collapse.

Ray finally stepped back. "Alright. Okay. We'll try ourselves." He gave a final look at the rubble and yelled out. "Bianca! If you can hear me! We're okay! We're going to continue on!"

---

Upstairs in the second floor offices, Bianca remained on her knees in her niece's arms. Her tears had run dry and Taylor's embrace had become the center of her universe. A safe place from the years of anguish... And then, ever so faintly in the distance, she heard Ray's final call. "We're going to the evidence room."

Bianca slowly pulled away from her niece and looked over at the stairwell door. "Did you hear that?"

Taylor didn't answer.

Bianca rose to her feet. "That was him. That was the prisoner. He's alive down there." Bianca started to the stairwell.

"Wait, Auntie Bianca."

Bianca paused and looked back at her niece. The little girl stepped toward her. "Don't do it."

"Do what?" Bianca asked, puzzled.

"Help him."

Bianca studied the worried little girl, then smiled reassuringly. "Oh no, honey. He's trying to help us. He can get rid of the bad one."

"No... No, he won't," Taylor insisted.

Bianca grew concerned and stepped back to her niece. "What do you mean?"

"He's not who he says he is. He's a liar. He lied to you about sending Danny back. He just wants to open the door so he can bring all the other bad things back from the other side. He'll be stronger than before."

Bianca struggled to make sense of what the little girl was saying. "Him? How do you know this?"

The little girl paused and took a shaky breath, then continued. "It's inside him... the one who took me from the school. The one who took me to that place. The one who did bad things to me."

Taylor's words cut deep; she hadn't considered the possibility that Ray could be inhabited by that monster. Her mind began to race back over everything Ray had told her. It was all his explanation and there was nothing to say that he was telling the truth. Everything they saw and heard together could have been his doing. There would be no way of actually knowing if the entity had possessed him like it did to Charlotte.

Tears began to rise in the little girl's eyes. "Please Auntie Bianca, please... Don't let him bring the other bad things here."

Guilt churned up inside Bianca; she reached out to Taylor and pulled the crying girl close. "Shhh... honey, okay... it'll be okay.... I'll do what I can... I promise."

———

Ray carried a heavy piece of concrete as he and Danny walked quietly down the basement hallway. The rubble was Ray's answer to opening the evidence cage. They reached the corner near the evidence room, and the little boy suddenly stopped.

"What is it?" Ray asked. He could tell the boy was sensing something. "Is it near?"

Danny slowly turned back to his father. "It's with her."

"The policewoman?"

Danny nodded. "It lied to her. It convinced her that she should stop you."

Ray considered the revelation. It made sense; that was how it always fought back. "Where are they?"

"Upstairs," Danny answered.

Then they would have time, Ray reasoned. There was no way Bianca could clear her way through that rubble before he could perform the Debhuihka and at least he knew it wouldn't be attacking them another way. "Okay, let's hurry."

Ray cut around the corner and down to the evidence room. He paused by the door, shifted the heavy chunk of concrete to his other hand and took a flashlight from his pocket. He looked back at Danny, then pulled the door all the way open and went inside. He reached back, closed the door after Danny entered, and twisted the lock closed. He knew the deadbolt wasn't much of a deterrent, but it would at least slow down Bianca when she got there.

Ray carefully counted the rows of evidence lockers, retracing his steps. It was at least six down he remembered. He paused, panned his light around and studied his surroundings.

*Yes. This is right.*

Ray cut down the row to the far end. There it was. The cage on the end. His backpack was still there. Ray put the flashlight in his mouth, lifted the chunk of concrete high over his head and brought it down with all his might. The chunk slammed on the cage lock with a loud *CLANG*. The edge of the concrete crumbled from the force.

But the lock remained stubbornly in place.

*Shit!*

Ray looked back at Danny. This was going to take some time.

———

Upstairs, Bianca pulled away pieces of rubble that covered the staircase leading downward. Her little niece stood in the shadows behind, watching her every move. "Let me help, Auntie Bianca."

"No, honey. It's too dangerous." Bianca pulled aside a twisted piece of railing; beneath it was a large concrete slab. She worked her fingers around the edges and pulled. Sharp pain shot up her arm from her wounded hand. "Ahhh..." She let go and cradled her aching hand. Bianca sat back, waiting for the pain to subside. "This... this piece is too big... I... I need another way to move it." She coughed on the rising dust, then picked up her flashlight that was propped on the stairs above her and started back to the second floor offices.

"Where are you going?"

"I'll be right back. I need something to pry it with." Bianca entered the second floor offices and panned her flashlight across the toppled furniture. She spotted the fallen bar bells and hurried over. She pulled up one end of the bar with her good hand and the weights slid off. She then tipped it the other way the rest fell to the floor. The bench press bar was heavy, but it was certainly strong enough. She carried it back to the stairwell.

Bianca came downstairs to the collapse. She propped her flashlight back on the steps above, and turned to the rubble...

The heavy concrete slab had been shoved aside.

Bianca looked down into the opening, puzzled. "How did that?..."

"I told you I could help." Taylor interjected happily.

Bianca looked back at the little girl, standing innocently behind her. It was impossible. There was no way that little girl could have moved the heavy slab; Bianca couldn't do it even if she had two good hands. "You moved it?"

The little girl nodded and smiled. "We need to hurry."

Bianca studied her niece in silence. Something wasn't right. "Honey... How did you do this?"

"Things are different for me here. It didn't seem heavy."

It took a moment for it to sink in; if Bianca had heard this a few short hours ago, it would not have made sense. But in the world she found herself in now, the explanation was strangely normal. After all, the little girl had crossed back over from the realm of death.

"Go on. I'll follow you down," Taylor urged.

Bianca finally looked away from the little girl. She picked up her flashlight off the steps, then crouched down and peered inside the dark opening. Her beam of light revealed a gap in the rubble big enough to crawl through to the basement below. Bianca eyed the passage warily "I don't know... It seems risky. It could collapse."

"It won't. You'll be fine. Promise," the little girl assured her.

Bianca looked back once more at Taylor. There was something oddly mature about her behavior. "Honey, how can you promise that?"

Taylor looked at her for a moment, and then a darkness clouded her little face; fearful tears began to well in her eyes. "Auntie Bianca, please. We have to hurry. We have to stop him."

And there it was again. The guilt Bianca felt as she looked into her niece's helpless, frightened face was palpable. She reached out and touched Taylor's arm reassuringly. "It's okay, honey. Don't worry. I'm going." Bianca turned back to the opening, picked up her rifle, then crouched down and entered the tight passageway.

# CHAPTER SIXTEEN

Ray fought to catch his breath as he leaned down and examined the cage lock. His relentless pounding against it was beginning to show signs of success. The lock was almost broken through. "This will do it," he said confidently. Ray picked up the concrete chunk, raised it high above his head and brought it down. It smashed against the lock and it sprung open. Ray sighed, relieved, and looked over at Danny who was waiting nearby. "Okay... Okay now... stay back," he panted.

Danny backed away and watched as his father pulled the cage door open. Ray reached into the evidence cage and grabbed his backpack. Rotting bile and blood dripped from it as he pulled it out and carefully lowered it to the floor. He unzipped it and reached inside. He coughed and turned his face away to avoid the foul odor; his fingers groped for the symbol until he found it. He slowly pulled it out...

*CRACK!*

A searing white light flashed from the center of the pentagram eye. Ray cried out and recoiled.

"Daddy!" His son yelled anxiously.

The symbol toppled from Ray's hand... but it didn't fall to the ground. Instead it began to slowly rise up, floating over the room. A rotting, dark breath exhaled from the center of the hoop.

Ray backed away, staring up at the hideous phenomenon; he had seen this before but never without invoking it first. It was much stronger now, empowered by forces from both sides of the divide.

Danny stepped up behind his father. "We have to start, Daddy."

Ray pulled his gaze off the symbol. He kneeled to his son and gathered him into his arms. "Oh God, I wish there was another way."

Danny hugged his father back. "I'll be looking for you."

"And you'll find me... one day, you'll find me again. I promise." Ray fought back his tears as he slowly pulled away from the little boy. He looked up at the floating symbol, then kneeled before it and closed his eyes. "Ne... nahii wi... Dua... Duganipe... Paitsi... Paitsi... Nean Dua..." As Ray began to whisper the words of the Debhuihka, the rotting, dark breeze exhaling from the center of the symbol began to slowly grow weaker.

----

Bianca strained as she pulled herself out of the narrow opening in the basement rubble. She slumped back, coughing on the dust that hung in the air. She turned and looked back up into the narrow passage. "Taylor!... Taylor, it's safe. You can come down!"

"I'm here, Auntie Bianca."

Bianca spun around, startled. The little girl was already in the hall behind her. She smiled sweetly. "Come on."

Bianca watched her niece start off down the hallway; this was just another reminder to Bianca that she was dealing with a very new reality. Bianca pulled herself to her feet, picked up her rifle, and followed. They passed the holding cells, turned the corner, and crossed down to the evidence room. Bianca gave the knob a try. It was locked, just the way Ray had left it.

"He's already started," Taylor said.

Bianca pulled the key ring from her belt. "I'm hurrying."

*Click.*

The door lock sprung open on its own. Bianca hesitated, then looked back at Taylor. The little girl was holding the rifle out to her. "It's too late for anything else now. This is the only way to stop him."

Bianca stared at Taylor for a moment, struggling with the sight of such an innocent-looking child with a gun insisting that she kill Ray in cold blood.

*Could she be wrong about all this?*

And then Bianca heard it, clear as day in her mind...

*How could you doubt me? After you left me to be killed by that monster.*

Hearing Taylor's chilling voice in her head overwhelmed Bianca with renewed guilt; her doubt evaporated. Of course she would shoot this monster. She'd shoot him. Stab him. Beat him to death if she had to. Whatever it took to destroy him. Bianca took the rifle from Taylor, quietly opened the door, and slipped inside.

Across the evidence room, Ray remained on his knees whispering his incantation below the floating symbol. "Ne... nahii wi... Dua... Duganipe... Paitsi... Paitsi... Nean Dua..."

The rotting breeze grew weaker and weaker until it finally died into stillness. Ray remained motionless with his eyes closed. And then...

A breeze began to suck back in the other direction, into the center of the symbol. Ray opened his eyes and looked at Danny. "It's time."

Bianca crept around the end of the rack, just in time to see Danny walking toward the symbol.

"Hurry. Now." Taylor whispered urgently to her.

Bianca raised the rifle and drew down on Ray. Her finger moved to the trigger...

At that same moment, Danny sensed their presence and looked over. "Daddy!"

Ray spun around.

"Do it!" Taylor screamed in Bianca's ear.

And then everything seemed to happen at once: Bianca pulled the trigger. Ray took a dive. The bullets ricocheted off the rack above him.

Bianca rushed around the edge of the rack for a clean shot. But Ray leapt out and tackled her. They crashed to the floor. The rifle skittered under a metal rack out of reach. Bianca's training instantly kicked in. She flipped Ray onto his back, slammed him to the floor, and jammed her forearm across his throat.

Hatred blazed in Bianca's eyes. "I know who you are."

Ray looked up at her desperately. "Wha... whatever she told you is a lie."

Bianca leaned in harder against his throat.

Ray pushed back with all his might. "I... I warned you... he'd try to trick you." Ray twisted his head to the side, avoiding Bianca's direct pressure on his neck. He grabbed her wounded hand and squeezed.

Bianca cried out in pain.

"That's not your niece. It's him. He's using you. As long as I control the symbol, he's powerless against me." Ray insisted.

The stale breeze began to gather force, sucking back into the eye of the symbol. Bianca looked over at Taylor. Tears streamed down her little face.

*Hurry, Auntie Bianca. He'll come for me again if you don't.*

The little girl's thoughts stabbed cruelly into Bianca. She turned her attention back to Ray with a new determination. Ray squeezed her wounded hand harder, but Bianca fought through the pain. This was her chance to avenge Taylor's vicious murder.

Ray gasped. He knew he was almost out of time. He locked eyes with Bianca; he had to get through to her somehow. "Bianca, please... listen to me. When you first saw your niece... You didn't feel love, did you? It was guilt. All you felt was guilt."

His words were distant, but whatever small part of Bianca that was buried beneath her rage heard him. He was right. Guilt was what she felt when she saw Taylor.

*So what? What does it matter?*

Every day since Taylor was taken, she battled that guilt. It was her constant companion. Her blanket. Who was she without it?

"That's what it uses to destroy you. If you forgive yourself, it's powerless over you," Ray gasped.

Bianca hesitated. Was this a trick? In what possible way could Bianca ever forgive herself?

Taylor stepped in front of Bianca. *"He's lying. Don't listen to him."* The little girl stood her ground as the wind spiraling into the eye of the symbol raged around her. Her tearful voice was clear and present in Bianca's mind.

*Auntie Bianca... please... please.*

The searing wind intensified even more; the flesh on the little girl began to ripple unnaturally.

Bianca remained frozen at the sight of the bizarre image.

The rosy color in Taylor's face began to fade away. Tiny fissures began to split her delicate skin. The rotting blood and bile seeped from the wounds.

*Make it stop, Auntie Bianca... make it stop... look what you're doing to me...*

Bianca stared, horrified, as the little girl's flesh turned gray and started to sluff off her body, dissolving away and transforming into...

The emaciated gray man.

He let out an unearthly screech and grabbed Bianca's legs. She splashed down into the spreading swamp of rotting bile and blood, letting go of Ray.

Ray slumped back, desperately catching his breath. The wind howled back into the eye of the symbol as the gray man started clawing his way up Bianca's legs.

"Dirty little bitches," the gray monster growled angrily.

Bianca kicked and fought for her life. The harsh wind began to melt the gray man's translucent, bony legs into rotting blood. The horrific effect ran up his body until only his hands were left. The hands clawed their way up Bianca's chest to her throat and then they too dissolved into rotting blood. The repulsive ooze streamed down Bianca's throat. She coughed and gagged, fighting to breathe.

Ray struggled against the intense wind to reach Bianca, but it was no use. The massive steel racks toppled and crashed into one another; the walls trembled with the violent storm.

Ray looked over at his son, who began to pull apart, dissolving into the dark, hollow wind.

"Daddy..." He whispered, and then he swirled away into the black void.

Danny was gone.

Ray stared into the inky blackness; his ordeal was finally over. The balance had finally been restored.

Only it wasn't.

Instead of the void closing, it remained open and began to grow stronger. Ray grew troubled. This wasn't supposed to be the way it went. There was something else holding it open now. A new imbalance. Ray looked over at Bianca.

It was her. She was still yearning for Taylor; her guilt was keeping them connected.

Bianca started to slide toward the void. She grabbed hold of a heavy rack, but it was no refuge from the sucking wind. It groaned and scraped across the floor, heading toward the vortex. Bianca stared into the black abyss; tears began to well in her eyes. All of her pain began to flash before her eyes. The tattered hallway. The bathtub. Her niece. The small voice rang in her ears "You left me, Auntie Bianca... you left me."

Tears spilled down Bianca's cheeks. "Please Taylor... I'm sorry... I'm so sorry."

Ray yelled out to her, alarmed at the sight of her letting go. "Bianca! No!"

But Bianca's mind was somewhere else. Ray was wrong. She didn't have to forgive herself. She didn't deserve it. There was another way to put an end to her suffering; a way to punish herself for the final time. Bianca's grip slowly relaxed. She felt her fingers slip off the metal shelf and her body being carried away on the powerful wind rushing into the void. It would all finally be over...

*WHAP!*

Bianca felt a penetrating slap on her arm. Her body was suddenly jerked to a stop.

It was Ray, desperately clutching to her, preventing her from being pulled into the void.

*BOOM!*

The void collapsed with a deafening explosion. The wind instantly died into silence. And the symbol fell to the floor.

Bianca tumbled to the ground in a daze. She remained there for a moment, catching her breath, then looked over at Ray, crumpled on the floor nearby.

He had saved her life.

# CHAPTER SEVENTEEN

The entire station was engulfed in flames by the time the first fire truck arrived. They joined the ambulances and other emergency vehicles in the parking lot. Helicopters circled the early morning sky.

The news stations from down below swarmed to the scene as well. Multiple live news reports were being filed, but they all related the same set of "facts:" The USGS pinpointed the epicenter of the 5.7 earthquake to be directly below the station. The violent tremor had triggered the fire in the generator room that had quickly spread. Bianca was the only survivor and she had provided the harrowing details of the disaster. Ray and the unidentified transient had perished in the holding cells. The two bodies were burned by the intense fire beyond recognition. The other officers had never made it out of the station.

Given the intense destruction, there would be little evidence that could counter Bianca's account. Yucca Valley was no stranger to violent earthquakes; the 1992 Landers quake had buckled roads and broken water mains. There was nothing unbelievable about what had transpired.

The fire had been Bianca's idea. It was a testament to how much her life had changed in just one short night; she never would have considered lying to an official before. After the void closed, Ray climbed through the rubble and retrieved the road flares from the office supply cabinet above. They used them to ignite the rotting diesel in the generator, then climbed out safely.

During her debriefing, the sympathetic detective thanked Bianca for her professionalism after she had insisted on telling her story before they took her away to the hospital to stitch up her hand. But for Bianca, it was a matter of life and death. She needed her story to be the record of fact if there was going to be any chance for Ray to avoid capture. After everything he had done for her, it was the least she could do.

In the days that followed, Bianca found that coming down from the adrenaline of that night proved a much harder endeavor than creating the false story. Everything seemed so ordinary. There was no one she could talk to about it. She had to live her lie.

Bianca would forever be gauging events in her life based on the horror she had witnessed. It was PTSD in the extreme. She had fundamentally been changed; everything she believed about life before that night had to be re-evaluated. Sounds in the night, coincidences, strange crime scenes, and ranting crazy transients that she once wrote off, could never be taken at face value. Knowing there was another level to the life we all accept could never be ignored again. And no one could know. It was a new companion to her guilt.

———

Ray retreated to the low desert where he greeted each morning's sunrise standing at the entrance of his cave. He had returned to The Family. No one asked where he had gone and no one questioned his return. Just like before, he asked no one's name and no one asked his. It was exactly what Ray wanted. What he needed. This was his home now.

He managed to return to the simplicity he had found when he was staying there before. He had shed his clothes much sooner this time and he found the rhythm of life there reassuring. There was nothing else he wanted. The part of him that had been burning inside had quieted. He had let Danny go. He would never feel complete again, but he could at least continue.

After several weeks, Ray even began to go on the spiritual sojourns into the box canyon for the rituals the women elders performed. Rituals that acknowledged but also appeased the balance between the two sides.

Equilibrium never felt so good to Ray. It was all about harmony. There would be the occasional visitor, just like Ray had been. He could sense their anxiousness and their imbalance. But, just like the others in the commune, he said nothing. He knew they were on their own journey and would either find what the sought or they would leave, unsatisfied.

Ray knew he had to commit to this way of life, even when he found himself occasionally thinking about Bianca. He knew he could never see her again. He had originally gone to her out of desperation, hoping she would believe him, and in the end, she had. He liked to believe that she had finally found some peace of her own, but there was always something in the back of his mind that nagged at him. He had saved her life, that was true, but he had only physically saved her from the void. She had never actually let go of her guilt, and that meant she was still holding on to her niece and the other side.

---

It had been several months since the incident. Bianca had gotten her head back into a place where she could function. She was offered her job back in San Bernadino and she accepted. What else was she going to do? At least it was something she was familiar with. She had even managed to keep her drinking in line so far.

It all seemed to be working for her until the night her life took another turn...

After a long day at work, Bianca was curled on her bed in her rental house in San Bernadino. She kept the TV on at night even as she slept. Something about the noise was a comfort after everything she'd been through. She had finished her second glass of bourbon and was considering turning out the lights when she hesitated.

She had yet to reach out to her sister. She knew she had to at some point but just couldn't seem to get into the right frame of mind. Bianca looked over at her cellphone charging on her nightstand. It was late. The odds of her sister actually taking the call were slim and that was good. She reached over and picked up the phone. If she just left a message, maybe that would be a good start.

Bianca punched up her contacts, and that's when she saw it: "Jim." She froze at the sight. She had never thought to delete his name and information. And now, something about seeing it made her feel that he was still there on the other end and all she had to do was reach out. Bianca stared at the sight for a moment in silence, and then tears welled in her eyes. Another unresolved emotion was rising to the surface. He had been so kind and patient with her. She had pushed him away as she often did to men. But now she felt she might have missed something special... What if she had been able to accept what he was offering her? What would her life look like today?

She stewed in this melancholy emotion for a moment, then blinked back her tears. Her finger moved to the options on her phone, then she hit "Delete," and his number disappeared from her phone and from her life forever.

Bianca considered her original intention to leave a message for her sister but decided against it. There was always tomorrow. Maybe she would find a time that felt right. She put the phone down, clicked off her light, and she sank back into her bed. She laid there for a long moment until her eyes grew heavy and she closed them.

The television sound faded into the distance as she approached sleep, and then it happened...

A faint little voice drifted to her from far away.

"Biaaan... caaa..."

Bianca's eyes snapped open. There was no mistaking her niece's little voice.

Bianca bolted up, her heart thundering in her chest. She turned off the TV and waited, listening carefully. And then it happened again...

"Biaaan... caaa..."

At that moment it was clear that this was far from over for Bianca.

# ABOUT THE AUTHOR

 Award winning writer/director John Penney attended UCLA where he studied film and received a degree in English. In addition to his screenplays, John has written short stories that have won him an award from the Adelphi Academy in New York, and have been published in the "Magazine of Fantasy and Science Fiction."

In 2011 John wrote and directed the supernatural thriller "Hellgate" starring William Hurt and Cary Elwes. The film was awarded Best Film at the Bram Stoker International Film Festival as well as the Best Horror Film from the Fantasy Horror Awards in Italy, sponsored by Syfy Europe Universal. Prior writer-director credits include the thriller "Zyzzyx Road" starring Katherine Heigl and Tom Sizemore, the family film "Magic" with Robert Davi and Christopher Lloyd, and a segment in the anthology film "Virus of the Dead."

In 2017 John formed the genre company Dark Arts Entertainment with Brian Yuzna, ("Re-Animator" "Honey I shrunk the Kids") which has been producing a range of quality, marketable features and multimedia projects, tailor made for today's discerning horror audience.

John is also currently prepping his next feature film, "Crossover," based on his novel "Truck Stop" and co-writing the final sequel to the seminal genre film "Re-Animator" for The Wolper Company.

In addition to his directing, John has written the screenplays for such films as "The Enemy" starring Roger Moore, Luke Perry, Olivia

D'abo; "Contaminated Man" starring Peter Weller and William Hurt; "A Breed Apart" with Robert Patrick, Andrew McCarthy; "In Pursuit" with Daniel Baldwin, Claudia Schiffer, "Matter of Trust" with C. Thomas Howell. "The Kindred" with Rod Steiger, "Return of the Living Dead 3" with Mindy Clarke, "Past Perfect" with Eric Roberts, Laurie Holden and "Amphibious 3D" with Michael Pare.

John also served as a producer on his films "Zyzzyx Rd" , "A Breed Apart", "Matter of Trust" and "In Pursuit" and Executive Producer on the feature "Reborn" (2019) with Barbara Crampton, Chaz Bono and Peter Bogdanovich.

In 2012 John wrote his first novel "Truck Stop" and followed that up in 2013 with his second novel, "Killing Time." His third novel is "It Comes Back." He is also featured in the book on screenwriting by Jose Prendes, "The High Concept Massacre" along with fellow screenwriters Carl Gottlieb ("Jaws") Amy Holden Jones ("Mystic Pizza" "Indecent Proposal") and Doug Richardson ("Bad Boys" "Die Hard 2")

John has been an adjunct Instructor at The Los Angeles Film School since 2013 where he teaches writing and directing.